Arizona Bride

PATRICIA BULLOCK

SCRIPTOR HOUSE
THE EPITOME OF GREATNESS

Scriptor House LLC

2810 N Church St Wilmington, Delaware, 19802

www.scriptorhouse.com

Phone: +1302-205-2043

© 2024 Patricia Bullock. All rights reserved.

No part of this book may be reproduced, stored in a retrieval system, or transmitted by any means without the written permission of the author.

Published by Scriptor House LLC

Paperback ISBN: 979-8-88692-231-8

eBook ISBN: 979-8-88692-232-5

Because of the dynamic nature of the Internet, any web addresses or links contained in this book may have changed since publication and may no longer be valid. The opinions expressed in this manuscript are solely the opinions of the author and do not represent the opinions or thoughts of the publisher and the publisher hereby disclaims any responsibility for them. The author has represented and warranted full ownership and/or legal right to publish all the materials in this book.

This book is dedicated to my son Aaron

My Angel in Heaven

April 1, 2023

As Erica pulled out of the driveway and headed out of town, she was full of excitement for her future. A month ago, she graduated college as a clothes designer and is now starting a new chapter in her life and praying that everything works out the way she hopes. Erica graduated from the university with top honors and Professor Lyons and Lulu came to see her get her diploma and to celebrate.

Lulu taught her how to sew and helped teach her how to design wedding dresses and special occasion dresses. She helped her with her portfolio and make samples of her designs, Lulu taught her how to be confident in herself and her work. Erica had always been interested in design school and loved remaking older clothes into new outfits and hoped to work for a famous designer someday. Erica grew up in foster care and most of the time she wore hand me downs that didn't always fit so she would cut and sew and improve them to fit her better. She would fix up the other kids that were there also because foster kids didn't always get what was needed. Erica would try to help the other kids when they needed clothes, especially the younger ones, but then they would just send her away, said she was causing trouble.

Erica lived in an abandoned car when she was 16 and after graduating from high school, and after starting college a friend let her live in her car the first couple of semesters then one day, she answered an ad for a job taking care of a professor wife who had ALS, she met with Professor Lyons and his wife Lulu and got the job. They were very nice, and Lulu was amazing, so smart and caring and easy to work for. She moved in and took care of Lulu and went to college full time. She had good grades and Lulu taught her to sew on a machine and helped her with her designs.

She learned so much from Lulu in those three years working and living there, that she could never repay the kindness and support that they showed her. After graduation Lulu called in some favors and set her up an interview with **The House of Jarrod** in Phoenix Arizona.

She had saved up all her money and bought a car and packed all her dresses she had made that she designed and loaded her car and headed to Arizona to start a new life, but she would truly miss Lulu and the professor. They have become her family and taught her so much and she is so grateful to have met the professor and Lulu. After saying her goodbyes, she headed out to Arizona from Louisville, Kentucky.

She traveled several days driving through Tennessee and Missouri, where after staying the night, lost her phone and had to go and get it replaced. Then of course her trip got even better, had a flat tire in Oklahoma and had to drive on it to get help, but the shop had closed so had to stay the night there and get it fixed the next morning. Then drove through Texas and stopped at Amarillo and decided that I had plenty of time to site see which was great, then driving through New Mexico drove through a dust storm which was scarry and finally in Arizona almost to my destination when the car breaks down.

Ericka was sitting on the side of the road praying for anyone to stop and help her, it had to be 100 degrees in Arizona in early June and all kinds of people have passed by, but none has stopped. After two hours deciding the next step is to get somebody to stop, so I striped off my white button up shirt that I had on and striped down to my camisole and rolled up the waist of my shirt to show my legs hoping some idiot of a man would stop and help me before I pass out in this damn heat. I undone my hair that I had put up in a nice bun for my interview and let my long hair down then I put my jacket on top of my trunk and hopped up and cross my long legs and smiled and fanned myself with a magazine looking like I couldn't do anything without the help of a man and sure enough a car stopped.

A big Black SUV pulled up behind my car, a handsome man around his mid thirty's got out dressed in a suit and tie. Great why couldn't a guy in a t-shirt and jeans stop and help I thought, he doesn't look like he could work on a car.

He walked over and he looked at the car then at me and said, "It's 100 degrees out here, are you having car trouble or trying to pick out your next John?"

That made me mad with his flip attitude, I said, "No just sunbathing, of course, I'm broke down you idiot."

"Cute if you don't need or want my help, you go back to sunbathing, but it looks like you already got plenty of sun already." he said with a smirk and turned toward his car.

"Ok fine, Yes I'm having car trouble, can you help me or not?" I said being catty then thought about it and smiled, "I sorry, I could use your help."

"Ok, where do you live?" He asked.

"In Kentucky." I answered.

"Well, I can't give you a lift that far but I'll take you in town and drop you off at the mechanic shop so you can get your car towed and fixed." He offered.

"Ok, thanks." I got my purse and grabbed my shirt and jacket and followed him to his car. After I got in, he reached in his door and handed me a bottle of water.

"Thanks, it's really hot here at this time of the year." I commented.

"It's always hot here, no matter what time of the year it is. Why are you in Arizona may I ask?" he asked.

"I came out about a job, and I missed my interview and as late as it is, I'm not going to get my car fixed fast enough to reschedule and get the job." I said.

"Where was your interview?" he asked.

"It was at Jarrod's, Designs Company in Phoenix. I'm a clothes designer, and it's hard to get a job like this in KY so I decided to relocated but it's not turning out like I thought it would." I explained.

"Things rarely do when you don't plan things out." he said.

"You're right, I should never have come here, this is the least friendly place I've ever been." I said.

"I've learned to depend on myself instead of others, then I know what to expect, I'm John Jameson."

"I'm Ericka Mann and really, thank you for your help. When I left to head out here, I lost my phone in Missouri, had a blowout and now my car breaks down in Arizona, 100 miles away from where I needed to be this morning, but I appreciate your help."

We pulled into a mechanic shop and John walked in with me and this nice-looking guy said, "Hi John, what brings you in?"

"My friend here broke down about 20 miles outside of Centertown, can you tow it and get it fixed for her."

"Sure, no problem." the man said.

"Ron this is Ericka Mann, Ericka this is Ron the greatest mechanic ever, if it can be fixed then he's the man to do it." John said.

"Thanks man, I appreciate that, Ms. do you have your keys and what kind of car is it?" Ron asked.

"A lemon apparently, I just bought it two weeks ago, it's a red 2015 Ford focus." I said smiling.

I handed him my keys and Ron said, "The hotel next door isn't great but there's a bed and breakfast about a block away that's nice. Just tell Millie that I sent you."

"Ok I will and thank you. Do you know when you'll be back with my car, my luggage is in the trunk" I asked Ron.

"No problem when I get back, I'll bring your luggage to Millie's as I head home this evening." Ron said.

"Thank you so much." I said.

"Hop in and I'll take you to see Millie, she a sweet woman you'll like her." John said.

"Ok thank you John, I really appreciate this." I said smiling.

"No problem, I just want you to be aware there are friendly folk here in Arizona." John said laughing.

Millie was a sweet lady in her early 60's and she took me in with no problem. When we got their John opened the front door and we walked into a beautiful foyer decorated in a southern charm with antiques and flowers, I thought maybe was a florist. John ring the bell and you could hear a sweet voice, "I'm coming, it just takes me a minute." And when she entered the foyer, she smiled and hugged John, "About time you come see me, where have you been keeping yourself?" Millie asked.

"I've been working." John said, "Do you have a room available for my friend Ericka, she broke down and Ron's gone to tow it for her."

"Of course, I do, I always have room for you and Ron and anyone you send me, I'll always make room." Millie said.

"Hello Ericka, I'm sorry you broke down but as they say everything happens for a reason. Come on in and I'll show you your room."

John walked upstairs with us, and we entered into a beautiful cream color bedroom trim with dark blue trim and beautiful cherry furniture. The bed had a blue bedspread with pink roses on it, with ivory lace curtains and fresh flowers. It was beautifully decorated and had its own bathroom.

"Thank you, Millie, I feel like a princess in such a beautiful bedroom." I said.

"We'll freshen up and come down when you're ready, I'll have tea and scones ready for you." Millie said. She and John walked out leaving me to sit down in a wood rocker with navy cushions and pink rose pillows sitting on it. I looked outside and there was a courtyard with a veranda and gazebo. Millie had roses and flowers in full bloom all the way around the courtyard. It looked beautiful out there, I washed my face and hands and brushed my hair and went downstairs to join John and Millie. Millie gave me a glass of iced tea and orange cranberry scones that tasted delicious, I just remembered that I hadn't eaten today, no wonder I'm so hungry.

John said, "I had better get going, I have work to do, I'll see you around, Ericka."

"Ok, thanks John for all your help." I said smiling and I watched him walk out the door and wondered if I'd see him again. Even though he was sort of rude at first, he seemed nice, and he had that handsome cowboy look going for him, he had dark brown hair and a nice tan, and you could see how well he was built through that grey suit he had on. And when he talked, he looked into your eyes and made you feel like you were the only one there. Boy I must be tired, fantasizing about John whom I've only known him for a few minutes.

Millie was great, we talked, and she told me all about the town, the shops and the people and around six, Ron brought my luggage and my box of samples of my dress designs.

Ron said, "I brought everything in your car in case you needed it. I check your car out and you blew the motor, tomorrow I'll check it out real close and I'll be able to tell you what it's going to cost to fix it."

"Thank you, Ron, I appreciate that, do you want me to go ahead and pay you for the tow tonight?" I asked.

"No, I'll have you a receipt tomorrow if you don't mind to wait." Ron said.

"No tomorrows fine thanks." Erica said, "If it can't be fixed reasonably is there a car sales place in the area?"

"Yes, there's Lawsons auto sales, he's reasonable and honest but let me check your car out first before buying something else." Ron said.

"Ok, thanks." Erica said.

Ron helped me and Millie carry my things up to my room and then he kissed Millie on the cheek, "I'm going home to check on Sherry, see you tomorrow." and he left.

"Who's Sherry, his wife?" I asked.

"No, his daughter, his wife passed away in childbirth. Sherry's almost three and quite adorable, she has everyone wrapped around her finger especially Ron and John." Millie said, "She usually stays with me in the afternoons later in the week, so you'll get to meet her, she just so sweet and loving."

I opened my luggage and started putting my things away in the dresser and I unzipped my huge suitcase and pulled out my wedding dresses and samples of other dresses I designed and made, and Millie helped me hang them in the closet.

Millie looked surprise, "Those are beautiful but why so many?"

"These are my designs, I'm a clothing designer, I was on the way to an interview in Phoenix when I broke down." I explain the whole thing to Millie, and she sat there and listen then she asked, "Don't your family miss you?"

"I don't have any family, Millie; I was raised in the system. I was in seven foster homes from the age of seven to seventeen. I worked hard in school and put myself through college while I lived in a car until I met a professor that hired me to help take care of his wife. They let me stay at the house to finish school and I help take care of his disabled wife Lulu. She has ALS and when she saw my designs, she said if I was going to make it in this world then I needed to learn how to sew and have samples to show off my craft, so she taught me how to sew and she helped me with my portfolio and she encouraged me to follow my dreams." I explained. "She came to see me when I graduate, and she help me send out my resumes and she knew Robert Jarrod, of Jarrod Wedding Designs and that's how I got my interview."

"She sounds like a wonderful person; I've always believed that everything happens for a reason and that the hardships we go through make us who we are meant to be in life." Millie said.

"Yes, I believe the same thing, I remember before I was taken away from my mom she told me, it is what it is, it's up to you to make life what you want," said Erica.

"How did you wind up in foster care if you don't mind me asking?"

"She overdose on heroin, and I don't know if she lived or not, they took my father to jail because apparently, I had drugs in my system, after he traded me to his dealer for drugs. I know nothing of him or her other than their names and that don't mean a thing to me." Erica said.

Millie said, "I'm sorry you had such a rough life, but you sure turned it around and these dresses are beautiful. I don't think I've ever seen anything so beautiful in my life."

"Thank you, Millie, I appreciate that, I love designing for each individual woman, I like to know her likes and dislikes so that her wedding dress will be so special that she'll want to pass it down to her daughter or daughter in law to be."

"I had better get downstairs and check about what to do for dinner, you rest and come down whenever you want." Millie said.

"I will, thank you Millie." I felt lucky to be here and to meet such wonderful people today. After Millie went downstairs, I washed up and change into clean jeans and a white t-shirt that had paw prints on the back of it and a bride and groom Pomeranian dogs on the front in wedding dress and tux that I made in my spare time. I sat down and wrote in my journal. Then I went down to see if Millie needed any help.

"Millie, do you need any help?"

"No dear, since it's just the two of us, I order pizza and it should be here any time." Millie said.

"Pizza sounds good, it's one of my favorites." Millie got glasses of ice and put sweet tea in them and carried them to the front porch. I followed her, and we sat on the porch and ate, and watched people walking down the street.

Millie told me about the history of town and the people that stated the town, and we had a great time. Millie told me if I wanted dessert there was an ice cream shop about a half block down the street that carried all kinds of sweets so I ask her if she wanted to walk with me but she said no, she needed to tidy up before it got late so I walked down the block there was the cute park and they had swings and tee totters and statues of children playing and there was quite a few kids playing at eight o'clock at night, but it being June I guess school out for the summer so I walked on pass the park and walked by several shops and boutiques including a bridal shop with a white wedding dress in the window with white flowers and white pearls and all the decorations was white which really clashed I thought, you couldn't really distinguish the beauty of anything it just all faded together in white.

The ice cream shop was right next door, so I walked in and sat down, a young girl, probably 16, waited on me. I ordered apple pie and coconut cake to go and while I was waiting, I was staring at the bridal shop when someone cleared his throat, I looked up and it was John standing there.

"Well, hello, I see your making your way around town." he said smiling.

"Yes, I'm managing I decided to come get dessert for me and Millie would you like to join me?" I asked smiling big.

"With that smile, how can I refuse?" John said laughing and he sat down across from me. "I got a call from Ron, he had an emergency and had to leave for a few days, he said if you couldn't wait tell he got back, we could have you towed to Charlies Shop, it's up to you."

"I can wait, I really like this town, and everybody is so nice, I hope it's nothing serious for Ron. Millie told me it's just him and his daughter."

"It's his mother-in-law, she fell and broke her hip, so he went to Phoenix for her surgery." John said.

"He's going to have his hands full with a little girl at the hospital." Erica said.

"He didn't take Sherry with him; I'm picking her up from the babysitter in an hour and I'll be taking care of her till he returns." John said.

My eyes must have gotten big because he smiled, "I've taken care of Sherry before, usually on the weekends when I'm not working, you do what you need to do." John said.

"You and Ron are close, have you known him long?" I asked.

"Yes, we were neighbors growing up and when our parents loss custody of us, we went to the same group home and I'm a year older than Ron, so I protected him from being bullied, and we became brothers." John explained.

"I'm sorry, but I know what that's like, I was put in foster care at seven because my parents preferred drugs over me and had been in seven foster homes tell I was 17 then I went out on my own." Erica said.

"Wow how did you get to leave before 18?" John asked.

"The foster home I was in didn't care if I was there or not as long as they got money for me, so I lived in a car that was broken down and I worked and finished high school, then I went to college and lived in the car for two semesters when a very nice couple help me and here I am at 22 trying to make a name for myself."

The girl brought my desserts and John walked me to Millie's, he told me about the park and about the town some and as we got to the front porch Millie came out and said, "John, Lucy called and she on the way here to bring you Sherry after she picks up Sherry's medicine from the pharmacy, so come in and wait."

"Ok" we went to the kitchen and Millie fixed hot tea to go with the cake and pie and we had our dessert and I asked, "Why is Sherry taking medicine, is she sick?"

"No, she has asthma and gets breathing treatments three times a day." John said.

Millie said, "John, why don't you leave her here so that I can take care of her while you work?"

"I cleared most of my schedule except Thursday afternoon and Friday morning, I have a two-hour meeting I can't reschedule but I'll bring her by those days if that's ok." John said.

"Yes, that's fine and you bring her by to see me tomorrow, maybe come for dinner tomorrow night." Millie said pleadingly.

"Ok, dinner tomorrow night." John said then the doorbell rang, and this beautiful young red headed woman came in carrying Sherry who was sound asleep.

"Let me take her Lucy, I really appreciate you bringing her to me, I would have come and got her." John said.

"I know John, but I needed to pick up her medicine, I forgot today when I was in town. I got everything packed and you have a key to Ron's place in case you need it right?" Lucy said.

"Yes, thank you so much, oh and by the way, let me introduce you to Ericka, she broke down and will be here for a short while, Ericka this is Lucy. Ron's neighbor and part time babysitter." John said.

"It's nice to meet you" Lucy said.

"It's nice to meet you too" Ericka said.

Millie said, "Lucy has your sister, found a wedding dress yet?"

"No, not yet, we just haven't found the right one but we're going have to find it soon, Nora's getting married in September so she may have to just settle." Lucy said.

"Oh, don't do that, I know someone that makes beautiful dresses, she does an amazing job." Millie said.

Lucy said, "Who, I'm so worried that Nora will not find the right dress."

Millie said, "Ericka here, she designs wedding dresses, and she has some samples you could look at if that's alright, Ericka."

Ericka smiled, "Of course you can look, whenever you want."

"Can I look now, I know it's late but I'm really excited?" Lucy said.

"Sure, come on upstairs and I'll show you what I have." and Ericka and Lucy walked up to her room and Ericka pulled out the dresses for Lucy to look at.

Ericka was in heaven with Lucy complementing her designs and loving them, she really liked the ivory dress, but she wanted it in white then she fell in love with the bride's maid dresses. Lucy asked if she could bring her sister and mom over to see the dresses tomorrow afternoon, so we made plans and Lucy left.

Erick went back downstairs, and Millie was in the kitchen, "Thank you Millie, Lucy loved my designs so much so that she's bringing her sister Nora, and her mom over tomorrow."

"You're welcome, dear, you have talent and Lucy, and Nora are twins and have been having a hard time finding a dress to go with her red hair and she's so tall she just really been stressing, so thank you." Millie said.

"I'd give anything for her red hair, Lucy's gorgeous, are the identical twins?"

"No but close, both girls are beautiful, Nora just smaller built, were Lucy's taller and slimmer." Millie said.

"I know we'll come up with a dress for her." Ericka said.

John walks in and smiles, "I didn't know you made wedding dresses." John said.

"I didn't see you, I thought you had left already." Ericka said.

"No, I was checking on Sherry, she's sound to sleep." John said.

Millie said, "John, sense your off tomorrow, why don't you stay here tonight Sherry's already in her jammies so you could put her in the deluxe captain suite she can have the twin bed and you can have the queen bed; all you need to do is leave her door open in case she wakes in the night."

"If we stay the night then you have to clean it tomorrow in case you rent it out." John said.

"It's ok, I'm capable of cleaning my rooms, it's part of my business." Millie said.

Ericka said, "I'll help her clean the room tomorrow, you might as well stay."

John smiled, "Ok but it's getting late, I had better get princess into bed."

Millie and I put Sherry's thing in the room, and I pulled the sheets back and John carried Sherry and put her in bed and kissed her goodnight and tucked her in, I said goodnight and went to my room and Millie locked up for the night. I slept like a baby that night. I thought about John and how gentle he was with Sherry last night; he's going to make a great dad one day.

I got up early and showered and dressed into my best jeans with a tank top covered with a pale pink lace and a handkerchief hem that I made. I brushed my hair and put a light coat of makeup on then I went downstairs. Millie was in the kitchen cooking breakfast, so I helped her and then she sent me to knock on John's door. He answered dripping wet wrapped in a towel "Come on in, I'm going to get dressed before Sherry wakes up and he disappeared into the bathroom. I heard a little giggle, so I peeked into the side room and Sherry was sitting on the bed playing with her doll.

I walked over to Sherry and said, "Hi Sherry."

The little girl looked up her smile beaming, "Hi" she said then she held up her baby doll.

"I like your baby doll; does she have a name?" I asked her.

Sherry smiled and said "Dolly, but her dress has a hole in it." I sat down on the bed beside her and smiled, "Yes, it does, would you like me to fix it, and it will only take a few minutes."

Sherry said, "Yes please, do you live here?"

"I'm stay with Millie until I get my car fixed."

John said, "I see you two have met."

Sherry's eyes got big, and she yelled "Uncle John, you're here." and she went running into his arms he picks her up and swung her in the air and he hugged her and kissed her cheeks then he said, "Of course I'm here, you're staying with me while dad's gone to see nanny. I bet your hungry, let's get some food in our bellies." and he blew bubbles on her belly, and she giggled and wiggled and then he put her down, "let's get you dressed first, then breakfast." Shery said, "lets hurry up, I want pancakes."

I laughed, "I'll see you two at breakfast." and I went to my room, and I fixed her dolls dress, and I made her a baby blanket with some the material scraps that I carry with me when I travel. I went down to breakfast; John was just getting Sherry to settle in her seat, so I walked over and handed Sherry her doll and the blanket I made her. Sherry squealed and said, "You fixed her, yeah." and she jumped up and hugged me.

I hug her back, "your welcome but you had better get busy eating."

John said, "Thank you for that but you shouldn't have." he sounded irritated, but I just overlooked it and told him, "It was nothing; I always carry scraps of material with me, I just wanted to see her smile." Erica said.

Millie brought a big plate of bacon and sausage, with a platter of pancakes, she said, "Breakfast is on, now everyone let's sit and eat."

I went and poured my coffee while John fixed Sherry's plate, Millie and John talked while I sat there drinking my coffee and I ate a pancake with bacon as a sandwich then I excused myself and went upstairs to make my bed and straighten my room and I pulled out my portfolio to show Lucy, Nora, and her mom Mary when they come later today.

I went downstairs and Sherry was playing on the floor in the sitting room, and I went to find Millie to see if she needed any help. Millie was in the kitchen talking to John as she started to go in, she heard John say, "I don't want Sherry to get attach to her, I don't know who she is or what she wants, there's something off about her."

I turned and walked out the door and went for a walk around town, I had several hours before Lucy and the girls was coming, I stopped into the bridal shop and there was this older lady in there she asked, "Hello my name is Claire, can I help you?"

"No, I'm just looking, you have some beautiful dresses in here." Ericka said.

"Thank you, but I haven't sold a dress in six months, most of my inventory is old, I haven't had any new dresses in two years." Claire said.

"I'm sorry to hear that, maybe you need to update you line and dress up your windows some." Ericka suggested smiling.

"Girls today don't want store bought dresses, they want designer dresses, and I can't compete with that so I'm thinking about retiring this fall." Claire said.

"How long have you been in business?" Ericka asked.

"Almost thirty years, and I only closed for a month when my James died but these days it doesn't pay for me to stay open, most girls go to Phoenix or Flagstaff shopping for wedding dresses. At one time when I first open my store, me and my mother hand made every dress but then when mom passed away, I started to order dresses, but I did all the alterations myself, but I'm almost seventy and it's time I retire and travel some before my time comes to an end." Claire said.

"Do you have children and grandchildren to visit?" Ericka asked.

"No, I wasn't lucky enough to have children, but I want to travel, me and James talked about taking a cruise and traveling around the world." Claire said.

"We'll I hope you get to travel and relax and enjoy your retirement. I plan on going to Paris and France one day myself." Ericka said "We'll, I'll see you again, I'm sure."

"Yes, please come back by, you have a great day Miss." Claire said.

"I will and thank you, you have a good day too." Ericka said.

"Thank you, Miss," Claire said.

"It's Ericka Mann and it's nice to meet you, bye Claire." and I hurried back to Millie's to clean up before Lucy, Nora and Mary came.

Millie was sitting on the front porch drinking iced tea when I walk up, "I wondered where you went to, John was looking for you but when we couldn't find you, he took Sherry and went on out."

"I just wanted to explore town and get some fresh air; did he say what he wanted?" Ericka asked Millie.

"No not really, he said something about apologizing for being rude to you." Millie said.

"Huh, I don't remember him being rude to me, oh well. Lucy, Nora, and Mary supposed to be here in about 30 minutes." Ericka said, "Oh and by the way, I stop in the bridal shop, and I met Claire the owner, she's really nice." Ericka said.

"Yes, she is, I feel sorry for her, she lost her husband about two years ago and she closed the shop for almost a month if not longer." Millie said.

"That's horrible, I can't imagine what she went through." Ericka said.

"When she lost James, she was devastated, he just dropped dead of a heart attack one night after dinner, he sat down to watch TV, and she took him his dessert, but he was already gone, and she took it hard. They don't have any children, so she's all alone." Millie said.

"She said she's going to retire, close the shop and maybe travel some, but I feel sorry for her being all alone." Ericka said.

"I don't blame her, she put her whole life into that shop, then just to lose the man of her life, how could someone go on after that but that's what we do, we grieve and take the next steps to move forward." Millie said.

"I feel sorry for her being all alone but then I can't imagine ever finding someone that could love me, I don't know that I believe in that kind of love, not for me anyway." Ericka said.

"Honey don't sell yourself short, you're a great person and beautiful and you have this caring and kindness that draws people to you." Millie said, "And here comes Lucy, Nora and Mary, I'll fix them tea and if you want you can bring all your dresses to the sunroom there's plenty of light and they'll be more comfortable in there." Millie suggested.

"Ok that sounds great, thanks."

Lucy walked up, "Hi Millie, Nora, Mom this is Ericka you have got to see her dresses, they are beautiful."

Ericka said, "Thank you Lucy, why don't you all have some tea and I'll bring all the dresses to the sunroom for you."

Mary said, "That would be wonderful, I hate stairs."

So, while Millie entertained them, Ericka ran upstairs and brought her six wedding dresses down, her portfolio and her four brides maid dresses and two maid of honor dresses down and hung them up around the room, then I went to get them to come check them out. Ericka walked into the sitting room and said, "I have everything ready for you girls."

"Great come on mom, you come too Millie please we want your opinion too." Lucy said.

They came into the sunroom, and they just loved the dresses, all my samples are size 6 to 12 because most are adjustable, she tried on several and fell in love with my ivory low-cut front and back with the matching hat with the veil made on to it. Nora tried it on, and the Ivory color looked great with her red hair, it had lace over the bodice and down the skirt area and it had a slight train on it.

Mary said, "I think we found the right dress."

Lucy said, "Yes we did, how long it will take you to make Nora's dress?"

"About six to seven weeks but I have to find a place to sew and make it but I'm up to it if that the dress you want." Ericka said.

Mary said, "What if I ask my neighbor if you could use his garage to work in."

"No that's fine, I'll find someplace but you have to pay for at least half upfront and did you see any bride maids or mother of the bride dresses in my portfolio that you like." Ericka asked.

Mary said she wanted the lavender mid-calf length, so I did all the measurements and Lucy picked a dark lavender maid of honor dress, after measuring each one, Millie served tea and sandwiches. I worked up the prices of each dress then they paid half down, and I told them I'd get back to them with color swatches and fabrics in a couple of days. After they left, I was excited, I had almost three months to make six dresses, Nora's wedding dress, Mary's dress, two bride maids, one maid of honor dress for Lucy and a flower girl dress, I can do it in plenty of time and I was so excited.

I asked Millie if she knew of anywhere where I could rent a small shop to make the dresses and she suggested that I go talk to Claire, maybe I could rent her sewing room in the back of the shop, it would help both me and Claire. I got so excited that I went on over to Claire's to talk to her about it. I went in and Claire was sitting there just staring into the mirror buy the dressing rooms.

"Excuse me Claire, are you ok, you look sad." Ericka said.

"No, not sad, just thinking about the past." Claire answered, "You're back already, everything ok?"

"Yes, it's great but I wanted to talk to you about business if you have time." Ericka said.

"Oh, I have time, I haven't sold anything in a while and no one breaking my door down, so I have plenty of time." Claire said, "Come let's have some iced tea and I made lemon blueberry scones last night, come join me."

"Thank you, I would love that." Ericka said and followed Clair into a small kitchen with this tiny table by the window, so I sat with her while she poured tea and sat out a big plateful of scones.

"These look delicious" Ericka said biting into one, "There heavenly."

Clair smiled, "Thank you, I love to bake and at one time when me and mom opened this shop, we did the dresses, cakes, invitations, and flowers. It was like a one stop bridal shop; I really miss those days, but I'm ready to close shop and start living and seeing the wonders of the world."

"That sounds like a dream of mine, I design wedding dresses and all kinds of dresses really, and I was on my way to meet **Jarrod of Jarrod wedding designs** in Phoenix when my car broke down. I met a woman that can't find a dress anywhere because she has red hair and doesn't like anything she's found." Ericka explained.

Clair said, "Nora Johnson, yes, she and her sister Lucy have been trying to find the prefect dress. I sent her to Phoenix to Jarrod's boutique and she said the salesgirl was rude to her and told her she need to die her hair for the wedding. I felt so sorry for her to go through that, weddings are stressful enough without someone adding to it."

"We'll I'm glad that I didn't make it to my interview after all, weddings are about the couple but especially the bride. Lucy, Nora, and Mary came over to Millie's earlier today to see my designs and she picked out her wedding dress, her mom's dress, and several others. Millie suggested that I ask you if I could rent one of your sewing rooms for the next three months?" Ericka asked.

Claire smiled, "You look so excited, just like me when I started my shop, yes of course you can use it."

Ericka smiled, "Thank you Claire, how much for rent so that I can bring it to you tomorrow?"

"I won't charge you rent you can use it whenever you want, I'll even give you a key to the place that way if you want to work in the evenings, you could get in?" Claire said.

"No, I have to pay rent, I have to do this on my own for me, to make sure I'm cut out for business." Ericka insisted.

"Ok, if you insist, what about $ 50.00 a week plus you work in the shop Tuesday and Thursday mornings from 9 to 11 to help me out. What do you think?" Claire asked.

"You have a deal and thank you again Claire, I really appreciate it." Ericka said and gave her a hug.

Clair smiled, "You're very welcome, let me show you my sewing room and we will figure out if you need more space, I have extra rooms back there you can use if need be."

Clair showed Ericka the sewing room which was huge, and the extra rooms all had sewing machines and dress forms and worktables then she showed her the walk-in closets with every sewing notion fabric lace and silk flowers. Clair asked her, "Would like to come tomorrow around eight and start working, it being Thursday."

"Yes, that would be great, thank you Clair."

"Your Welcome, I'll see you tomorrow." Clair said, "And here is an extra set of keys so you can come and go as needed."

"Thank you" smiling, "I'm so excited see you in the morning." and headed to Millie's.

Then Ericka rushed back to Millie's to tell her the good news. She found Millie in the bedrooms freshening them for her guest coming tomorrow and Friday. Ericka helped Millie with the two rooms, then Ericka cleaned and changed sheets in the room that John and Sherry stayed in.

Millie said she tries not to rent that room in case John or Ron needs it, but she had a couple with a five-year-old coming Monday, so I got the room ready for her. Afterwards I found Millie in the kitchen cooking a full meal for John, Sherry, and me, so I helped her by cleaning up behind her and loading the dishwasher and wiping down the table and setting it.

The phone rang and it was Ron asking about Sherry and John, then when Millie got off the phone you could tell she was agitated so I asked her, "What's going on Millie, who rubbed you the wrong way?"

"I'm sorry but that was Ron, and he said his woman friend Chelsea is coming to dinner tonight, so that she can check on Sherry supposedly." Millie said.

"What's wrong with her, why don't you like her? I thought you liked everybody?" Ericka said.

"She has no interest in Sherry or Ron, it's just an excuse to see John." Millie said.

"If she interested in John, why is she seeing Ron?" Ericka asked.

"She's a gold digger, she tried to dated John and tried to talk him into going to California or New York to practice law because he would make great money and could have anything he ever wanted, but he told her this is what he wanted. So, she quite seeing him and moved on to Ron to make John jealous I think but when that didn't work, she found out about Sherry's trust fund and suddenly she loves children especially Sherry, she keeps telling Ron that Sherry needs a mom in her life, not an uncle like John." Millie said, "She's up to no good where Ron and Sherry are concern, and she has the hots for John, but he has no interest in her thank goodness."

Dinner was done and I help Millie put the food on the table when the doorbell rang, I went to answer it for Millie thinking it was John and Sherry but instead it was this somewhat beautiful woman in her mid-thirty's wearing way too much make-up and perfume and smoking a cigarette.

"Can I help you?" I said smiling instantly disliking this woman.

"I'm here for dinner with John and Sherry, I'm Chelsea, when did Millie hire a maid, I thought the old bat was too poor to hire help."

I smiled and said, "I'm not hired help, I'm friends with Millie and John." not sure why I threw John name in there but the look on her face showed that she's interested in John.

"Is John and Sherry here yet, I just love that little girl so much, I love her like a daughter." Chelsea said.

"No, they're not here yet, but you can wait for them if you want." Ericka said, "Would you like to join me and the old bat in the kitchen?"loudly.

"Sorry about that, it's just pet names we use for each other, I meant no harm." Chelsea said and followed me into the kitchen.

Millie looked up and said, "Hi Chelsea, John called, and he and Sherry can't come tonight."

"Well, that's rude; he knew I was coming to check on my precious girl. Well, I'll be going then." Chelsea said and turned and left without another word.

Ericka smiled and said, "She's something, I can say." and her and Millie burst out laughing.

John peek his head inside the kitchen, "What's so funny, is she gone?"

Millie said, "Yes, she's gone, I think when Ericka called her out on calling me an old bat, she was glad you weren't here."

"She called you that! Ericka next time Chelsea insults Millie, back slap her into the millennium. I'm a lawyer, I'll get you off, I promise." John said laughing.

"Ok then, I'll remember that where's Sherry?" Ericka asked.

Sherry jumped out from behind John, "I'm here" and ran over to Millie and gave her a hug then she ran over to Ericka and hugged her. Millie said it was time to eat so dinner we talked and laughed and had a great time.

During dessert, I told Millie and John about working and renting Claire sewing room and they were excited for me.

John asked, "How long would it take to make the dresses?"

"I have three months and two days so I'm starting tomorrow, and I'll have to put in long hours, but I can do it but I'm going to have to find somewhere cheaper to live for three months so if you know of a month-to-month apartment let me know." Ericka said.

Millie said, "You can stay here; I'll figure something affordable out for you."

"No Millie, you need to rent out my room and make a profit, but I promise I'll come and visit." Ericka said, "And I'm not leaving soon it'll will take a while to find something."

I helped Millie with the dishes while John and Sherry entertained us, then John said, "goodnight" and they left. I told Millie goodnight and went to bed excited for tomorrow. I got up early and showered and dressed in my light blue suit and white cotton and lace shirt, I put light make-up on and minimal jewelry and light blue sandals. Then I went and had coffee with Millie then I walked to Claire's shop. It was a beautiful day and I got there early, and Claire was already there, she showed me the basics and told me if I needed anything I could call her, and she gave me her number and explained she had physical therapy twice a week for her back that she hurt it in the spring. After she left, I cleaned up the shop and rearranged the displays and changed out some of the wedding dresses she had in the front window. A lot of the dresses were outdated and with some imagination could be revamped into beautiful dresses.

A young woman came in with a wedding dress that was her mom's that came from Claire's shop, she wanted to know if I could fit it and make it more her stylish. Claire came back when the young woman was there, so I introduced Sarah to Claire, she remembered her mother and got out a book that had pictures of brides that bought their dress from Claire's shop. Sarah was excited to see her mom's picture, so Claire gave her the picture of her mom. Then she asked if I could re-work the dress into what she wanted.

"Yes, I can, let's sit down and I'll make some notes on what you want."

Me and Sarah talked and decided on what she wanted and how to do it and I gave her the price and she went ahead and paid half, after she left, I told Clair, "That was a wonderful thing for you to do."

"We'll, I had plan on sending everyone's picture to them since I'm closing down, and it felt good to give Sarah her mom's picture." Claire said.

They had a good morning then Ericka cleaned the sewing rooms and organized them then she called and asked Claire who cleans and maintains or repairs the sewing machine, she said David Jones used to, but his daughter Heather took over and she gave me her number and that she had a sewing and fabric shop and that I could probably get the, all the fabrics and notions that I would probably need there.

So, I called Heather sewing shop to come and clean the sewing machines and they said they could come Monday morning. I got their address and decided to go visit and check out their store for fabrics and notions. I worked all afternoon and was surprised when it was six and Clair said goodnight, she'd see me tomorrow. I finished cleaning the small sewing room then locked up and headed to Millie's.

I got to Millie's, and she said she had me a plate in the oven so after I ate, I sat on the porch and talked with Millie. I asked her about sewing shops in the area and she told me about Heathers sewing shop and about a speciality fabric shop in Lansing about 15 miles away, then she said Phoenix had several shops. I got on my laptop and researched sewing shops to see what all they carried before I went shopping and the one in Lansing had the best fabrics for wedding dresses and special occasion dresses so I decided that I would rent a car and go shopping this weekend. I looked up rental cars and it was about 8 miles from Millie's, so I called, and they could pick me up so after I made the arrangements, I got ready for bed. I was just so excited about Sarah dress that I went downstairs and fixed me a cup of hot tea and sat down at the kitchen table and started sketching her dress. I worked on my sketches until midnight then I went to bed. I got up early and showered and dressed then I went to the shop before eight. I laid my sketches on the drawing table, and I looked at Sarah dress and sketch it as it is now then I made more sketches I had several designs done by the time Claire got to the shop at nine thirty she looked at the designs and said, "You are amazing, these are great, when are you calling Sarah to look at them?"

"Do you think their ready for her to choose?" Ericka asked.

"Yes, they are beautiful, I could see her in this design or that one or even this one here." Claire said.

"Ok, I'll call her and see if she can come in, thanks Claire."

"You're welcome my dear, you are truly gifted, now call her." Claire said as she went back to the front of the store. I called Sarah and she came over during her lunch break.

Sarah said, "I love them all, they all are beautiful."

"I'm glad you like them, is there one that stands out more that you like?" Ericka asked.

"I like them all but this one resembles the original dress more but with my style." Sarah said.

"Yes, that one I think fits your body style and yet matches you and your mom's original dress." Ericka said.

"Yes, that's the one I want, can you do it by the end of August, I'm getting married Labor Day weekend, my mom has cancer, and they think she only has six to nine months to live so I want her involved as much as possible." Sarah said.

"I'm so sorry about your mom and yes, I can get it done within a month and I'll help anyway I can ok." Ericka said.

"Thank you." Sarah said and gave Ericka a hug.

After she left, Ericka told Clair about Sarah mom and they had lunch together then the rental car company came, and I told Clair that I would see her Monday and left. After dropping off the car attendant, I drove to Lansing to check out Special Occasions Fabric Shop. The owner was there so I introduced myself and told her about what I was looking for and needed. She had an amazing choice of fabrics and sewing notions. She took me upstairs to where she kept all the wedding dress fabrics and lace. I felt like I was in heaven.

Heather helped me cut samples for Lucy dress and all the other dresses then I found some light pink satin and I gotten yards of it to take with me. I got ribbon and lace and thread and after I checked out, I stopped for dinner at Charlies Pub. I got seated and order a beer and steak sandwich while I was eating, I saw Chelsea walk in on the arm of a very handsome man and they were seated across the room from me, but I could see her hanging all over this man and they were kissing so I discretely snap a few pictures in case John needed them.

After I ate, I left the girl a tip and I went to Millie's, I got there around nine and Millie came running asking me to hurry. So I ran in the house and one of the guest was having trouble breathing and was having chest pain, and I told Millie to call 911 which she had already but they were tied up due to a wreck, so I help the gentleman to lay flat on the floor, he became unresponsive so I started CPR on him and one of the other guest hopped down on the floor to help me, I got a pulse and we could hear the sirens, I kept the CPR going tell the EMS got to him and took over, as the ambulance was pulling out, John and Sherry got there to check on everybody. I needed coffee so I was in the kitchen when John came in, "I hear you're a hero."

Ericka laughs, "Ha-ha, what are you doing out so late, where's Sherry?"

"I'm here," Sherry said from behind John.

"Hi Sherry, do you want a piece of cake with me?" Ericka asked.

"Yes please." Sherry said smiling climbing up into the chair at the kitchen table.

"Would you like a piece, John?" Ericka asked.

"Yes, I'm in, slice away." John said pulling up a chair.

"Where's Millie, I thought she'd come in here after everything happened." Ericka said.

"She's in with her guest reassuring them that George was doing ok because of you and that you knew what to do." John said.

"Ericka how did you know CPR, it's not something a clothes designer would know, would they?" John asked.

Sherry said, "I'm going to play, Uncle John."

"Ok sweetie, just stay out of everyone's way, ok." John said.

"I will" Sherry said and ran out of the kitchen.

"I learned CPR and first aid classes, one of the foster parents that I lived with sent me to take the class in their name, so they didn't have to." Ericka said.

John said, "That's terrible, I forgot you said you were in foster care, I'm sorry."

"It's ok, I made peace with it." Ericka said.

"What age were you when you went into the system?" John asked.

"Six almost seven, my parents thought drugs were more important, so they traded me to their dealer and when the dealer was busted, I was in the house. They sent me to the hospital, I had drugs in my system but then they found out I wasn't even his kid, so I was put in foster care after I got out of the hospital." Ericka said.

"I'm so sorry you had to go through that at such a young age, did you have a good foster home ever?" John asked.

"No not really, I had six foster homes until I was sixteen then I did CPR and first aid for Beth my foster mom when I was 15 then she expected me to work and give her my paycheck, so I moved into an abandon car down the street, and she said that as long as she got money for keeping me then I never had to come back. I work after school, and I finish high school with honors, went to college all the while living in car. One of my friends gave me their car to live in then I met the Professor, and he needed help for his wife she has ALS, so he offered me a job taking care of her and a place to stay. His wife Lulu, she's the one who helped me and taught me to sew, and we became really close. She's the one who set up my interview because she knew Jarrod but I'm ok with being here. I think I was meant to come here. I don't know if I believe in miracles, but Lulu always said when one door closes another one opens." Ericka said.

"Wow, you're amazing, to go through all that and to turn out with such a great attitude." John said.

"Well thank you, but I believe you have the ability to make life turn out the way you want if you're willing to work hard. I'm very happy, I have six dresses to make and one to redo, I feel very blessed." Ericka said.

"You have a great attitude, I'm really sorry I was rude to you when we first met, I'm just guarded around people." John said.

"Your fine, don't worry about it. Oh, by the way I have pictures of Chelsea with another man earlier tonight." Ericka said, handing her phone to John.

"That's her ex, supposedly he beat her and she's afraid of him. She doesn't look afraid now." John said bitterly.

"I'm sorry, I didn't mean to upset you." Ericka said.

"I'm not upset about her; it's what she's trying to do, she wanted to get involved with Ron to get her hands on Sherry trust fund and when I first met her, I had Sherry with me on an outing to the zoo and she thought I was Ron and tried to get involved with me until I explained that I was Uncle John. I tried to warn Ron, but he won't listen, and it just makes me mad that he's infatuated with Chelsea, and he don't want to hear the truth." John said.

"Sometimes people have to make mistakes and learn from them even if it's costly, you can't tell him who he can love but he's smart enough that he'll find out for himself before it's too late." Ericka said.

"I know but I don't want to see him hurt and especially Sherry, she's just a baby and after what me and Ron went through, Sherry deserves better." John said. Ericka started to ask what they had gone through, but Millie came in and hugged me "Thank you Ericka, I didn't know what to do and no one else knew either. I can't thank you enough." Millie said.

"You so welcome but anyone could do what I did." Ericka said.

"No, I didn't know but I will if it ever happens again, tomorrow I'm calling the Red Cross and set up CPR and first aid classes." Millie said.

"When you do, sign me up, my CPR certification will expire in September, and I want to keep it enforce." Ericka said.

John said, "Sign me and Ron up also, with having a child in our lives, it's something we need to know."

"Ok I'll take care of it tomorrow and thank you again Ericka." Millie said and hugged her again.

"You're welcome now, I'm going to bed, I have to meet with Lucy and Mary tomorrow and I may need to go shopping for more sewing things, night John, Millie, I'll see you in the morning." and Ericka went to bed and slept well.

The sun was shining when Ericka woke up and she smiled.

Today was going to be a good day she thought as she showered and dressed in jeans and t-shirt and tennis shoes. She went downstairs and Millie was in the kitchen cooking breakfast. Ericka asked, "Need help?"

"No, I'm almost done; I called the hospital and Mr. Clark is doing well, it was a heart attack, but his wife said if it wasn't for you, he would have died." Millie said.

'I'm glad I helped, I'm going for a run, and I need to stop by the shop then I'll be back." and Ericka left.

Ericka ran to the shop and went inside and got her sketch book with the designs of Lucy's dress and as she was leaving, she noticed a little girl probably around four or five sitting in the grass crying, so she walked over and said, "Hi sweetie what's the matter, where's your mommy at?"

She looked up with tears in her eyes, "she's in heaven" not knowing what to say or do, I sat down beside her, and she crawled in my lap and cried,

I held her close feeling her pain and almost cried myself. After she calmed down, I asked her "Where is your daddy or your grandparents."

She just looked up at me and pointed toward a little brick house down the block so I got up and took her hand and said, "I'll go with you, ok" and we walked across the street and down past two houses to the brick house, when we got to the front porch the little girl stopped and wouldn't move so I said, "Honey , you stay here and I'll be right back, Ok." and she nodded her head. I knocked on the door and yelled "Hello" several times, the wood door was open, so I opened the screen door and yelled again, then I stepped inside the house. I felt like something was really wrong, so I went on into the living room and on the floor was a woman. I could tell instantly that she was dead, so I turned to get out and I noticed behind the couch, there was a man who was also dead. I almost ran out screaming but I had to stay calm for this little girl. I stepped out onto the porch and the little girl was sitting on the sidewalk looking so lost.

I said, "Come with me sweetie and we will call for help." and we walked to the ice cream shop and it was closed but they were getting ready to open, so I knocked on the door and said, "I have an emergency." so the owner open the door and I told her, "I needed to use your phone" she looked at the little girl and said, "Come and sit down I'll get Donnie to get you something to drink" then she said, "follow me."

I told her what I found, and we called the police, and I called John. He said he would be there in a few minutes. The little girl name was Samantha and the police said both parents died of overdoses sometime last night. They were going to call social services, but I asked if she could stay with me, she was in shock, and I have been in similar situations so the police officer said that I could keep her for now until they find who her family is.

John asked me, "Are you sure you want to accept responsibility of this child, you know nothing about her."

"I know she needs me." I answered.

"Do you know anything about taking care of a child?" John asked.

"Yes, I took care of plenty of children in my time, and I won't let her down when she needs me." Ericka said, "Can you stay with her, and I'll go see if I can grab some of her things from her house?"

"You stay with her, I'll go and asked the chief, ok." John said.

"Thank you, John," Ericka said and smiled, and he smiled back at her and left. He came back about 15 minutes later, and he said, "The chief said they can't let anyone in yet."

"Ok, we'll can we leave yet?" Ericka asked.

"Yes" John said, "I told him where you were staying in case, they need to get in touch with you."

"Ok thanks" Ericka said then she went over to Samantha and said, "I'm taking you home with me, is that ok with you?"

Samantha shook her head yes and put her hand into mine and John drove us to Millie's.

Millie had heard what was happening, so she was prepared, she had some of Sherry's clothes and of course there were plenty of toys sense Sherry's there often. Millie fixed lunch and so we sat down, and I fixed Samantha a plate, but she picked at the food, and she didn't eat much. Sherry woke up from her nap and came in and she talked to Samantha, and they went to the sunroom to play. Millie asked, "Do you know anything about her family?"

"No Samantha doesn't talk a lot, I'm not really sure how old she is but I'm thinking four or five maybe. I can't imagine how she felt finding both her parents dead." Erica said, "She's in shock, I asked the police and EMS if I needed to take her to the hospital, but they didn't think she needed to go."

Sherry came running in saying "Sammy needs help" so we ran into the sunroom, and she was crying so I picked her up and held her and she finally fell asleep. I laid her on the couch in the sunroom and put a light blanket over her. The doorbell rang, it was Lucy, Nora, and Mary to see my designs. John sat in the sunroom while I was with them in case Samantha woke up. I showed them my designs for her wedding dress, and they were ecstatic over the dress then I showed her all the fabrics and lace, she asked my opinion, and I told her, I'd go with the ivory color satin and lace to match her red hair and she pick gold and silver rhinestone and pearls. Then with Mary's dress in lavender, I suggested a lavender hat with ivory netting then they picked out a dark purple maid of honor dress then light harbor mist which was a very pale lavender for the brides maid dresses and the flower girl dress was to match the maid of honor and they all was having hats to match their dress. The wedding is at the end of September, so I have plenty of time to get it done.

After they left, I checked on Samantha, she had woken up and was sitting on one side of John and Sherry on the other and John was reading to them. I stood there and watched, he was so good with children, and I could feel myself giving into those feeling that people call love, but I decided to fight those feelings because people don't really love each other, instead they destroy each other and then they have children and destroy their lives. I'm better off never having those feelings, I keep telling myself.

I gave Samantha a bath and put her in clean pajamas, I noticed bruises and scrapes and little red scars on her arms and legs like maybe burn marks so I asked her if I could take pictures of her legs and arms, and she shook her head yes. Then I took her down for dinner, she ate some, but she stayed by my side most of the time, John put a Disney movie in for the girls to watch and she sat on the couch with John and Sherry watching Lion King.

I help Millie with the dishes, "I'm sorry about bring Samantha here without asking you first, I just couldn't let them stick her in the system after what she went through."

"Don't you worry about it, we have plenty of room here, she's fine and I'll help you all I can." Millie said.

"Thank you, Millie, I don't know what I would do without you." Ericka said.

"Well, it's a good thing you don't have to know." Millie said.

After we got the dishes, all cleaned up there was a knock at the kitchen door, so Millie answered it and it was the chief of police James Martin, "Hello ladies, sorry to come so late but I have information on the little girl."

Millie said, "Sit down James, I'll get you a cup of coffee."

"Thanks Millie, I could use it, it's been a long and sad day." James said.

After Millie gave him coffee, he said, "Well the news isn't good, Rachel Harris and Roger Carter was the two that died last night but they weren't the girl's parents. Apparently, Rachel sister and husband died in an accident three years ago and Rachel being the only family they had, she got the child." James shook his head sadly, "And checking in to their history and Rachel's been on drugs for years and even lost the child once to social services in Alabama, that's why they moved here and that's where she met this, Roger Carter. We're checking in case there is family, but it looks like we're going to have to put her in the St Catherines Home of Innocence. Maybe someone will adopt her."

"No after what she went through, you can't do that." Ericka said almost in tears.

"I looked around in case I could get her some clothes and toys together but everything I found was rags and I found no toys or dolls. There was hardly any furniture in the house, a few chairs, and mattresses on the floor, garbage everywhere. That poor child was living in terrible conditions, and no one knew." James said.

"I gave her a bath she's covered in bruises and scrapes and red scars like burns, she let me take pictures and she said she was bad." Ericka said, showing James the pictures.

"I hate to say it but I'm glad they're dead and she survived that place, people like that don't deserve kids." John said.

"How could someone do that to a child, she a sweet thing and very frighten, she needs to be with people that care about her, not social services." Ericka said.

"I might not have a choice, we're a small town and we don't even have a place for children in this kind of situation." James said, "I can't do anything until Monday, so if you still want to keep her until we figure this out then that's fine with me."

"Of course, I want to keep her, I know what it like to go in the system and be passed around, the mistreatment and abuse you get, I just can't let that happen to Samantha." Ericka said with emotion.

"I'm caution you about getting attached to her, you're not even a resident here, you're just visiting, you have no roots here." James said.

"What if I ask for custody of her?" Ericka asked.

"If you tried to get custody of her, I don't know a judge that would go for it. I'm really sorry Ericka but if I find anything else out, I'll let you know." James said.

Millie walked James out and I sat at the table for a few minutes then I went into the living room, and I stood there watching the girls watch the lion king with John and they were laughing and having a good time, so I went back into the kitchen.

Millie came in and sat down with me, she patted my hand and said, "We'll figure something out, don't worry my dear, well ask John what we can do, after the girls go down for the night."

I shook my head yes and sipped on my coffee thinking about what I could do. John came in the kitchen and said, "Both girls are fast asleep on the couch, so I covered them up and sneaked in here, what are you two doing, you look serious."

Millie said, "It's serious, James came by, and Sammy has no family, the two that died wasn't her parents, the woman was her aunt. James said they probably will put her in the Home of the Innocence in Phoenix."

"Maybe she'll get adopted, you never know." John said.

"Maybe she'll get abused and neglected like most children that go into foster care." Ericka said as her voice broke, "I need some air." and got up and almost ran out the door. She sat on the swing in the back yard as memories from her childhood came flooding back and tears started running down her face then suddenly John was there holding her, and she turned her head onto his shoulders and just cried like a child herself. He held her until she quit crying then she looked up at him "I'm sorry."

"You have nothing to be sorry about, I know you had a bad time in your childhood but that doesn't mean that Samantha will, maybe the system will work for her." John said.

"I can't take that chance John, I love that little girl. I knew I will never marry because I don't believe in love, but this innocent child deserves a happy home with someone that loves her and I'm going to be that person will you help me?" Ericka asked pleadingly.

"I will help you but it's going to be a hard battle to win." John said.

"Thank you" Ericka said and hugged John and kissed him on the lips, a quick and light kiss but it was just enough for John to kiss her back and the sweetness of the kiss turned into passion and Ericka starting feeling things that she wasn't even sure what they were, she felt a needing for more and it scarred her, so she pulled away suddenly and blushed. John put his arms down, "Tomorrow we will figure out a plan if you're serious about keeping this girl, Ok?"

"Yes, I'm very serious and thank you John." Ericka said, still blushing.

"I won't sugar coat it, this will be difficult to do, and I can't guarantee we'll win but I'll do my best." John said.

"That's all I'm asking, we had better get in and check on the girls, have you heard from Ron?" Ericka asked.

"Yes, he's coming home Tuesday, his mother-in-law is going to rehab that morning then he'll be home." John said.

"I bet Sherry will be excited, she told me earlier that she missed her Daddy." Ericka said.

"Monday why don't we take the girls to the zoo?" John offered.

"That will be great." Ericka said as they went to the kitchen the girls were up and eating ice cream and cake. Samantha jumped down and ran over to me and grabbed my hand, "Will you sit with me?" she said softly.

"I sure will" and Ericka sat between Sherry and Samantha then after everyone had dessert, I suggested that it was bedtime and Samantha said, "Where's my box?"

And everyone looked at each other and I pick her up and said, "What do you need a box for?"

"To sleep in." Samantha said.

"Honey, we have a bed for you to sleep in." Ericka said gently and Samantha looked confused, "Mommy said I was bad, I have to sleep in a box like a dog."

"Well, I don't think your bad at all, you are going to sleep in a bed tonight and every night." Ericka said.

John said, "Millie do you still have a cot, we can put it beside Ericka's bed for Samantha, so she'll feel more secure."

"Yes, I do it's in the basement, can you go get it?" Millie asked.

"Yes, I'll bring it up and Millie if you get the bedding, I'll help Ericka makes it up for Sammy." John said.

Between Millie, John, and me, we got the cot up and made and Sherry wanted to sleep with Samantha, but John said that he would read them a story then they would see each other in the morning. Samantha was asleep before the story ended and Sherry said goodnight and John took her with him. Ericka crawled into bed and slept on and off in case Samantha needed me. Samantha slept all night probably from exhaustion from everything that happened yesterday.

Ericka woke up early and showered and dressed then went through her t-shirts and material and got out my sewing machine and made a pair of shorts and T-shirt for Samantha to wear, just until I could go out and get her some clothes. I had a blue teddy bear that Lulu gave me that came with a bottle of perfume, so I took the perfume off the bear and laid it with the clothes I made. It was going on eight, so I woke Samantha up and ran her a bath I help her wash her hair and wash off, then I help her dry off and Millie had given me a few pieces of clothes that guest had left, so I found underwear and socks and a pair of tennis shoes that fit her. Then I put her outfit on her and gave her the teddy bear and she hugged me and then we went down for breakfast. Samantha was quiet most of the time, the only time she talked much was with Sherry. I fixed her scrambled eggs, and I gave her sausage and bacon, she ate better this morning.

John and Sherry arrived around nine and they ate breakfast. The phone rang and it was Claire she had heard about yesterday and was calling to check on everything and she asked if she could come by after church, so I told her yes, we'd be here. The girls played in the sunroom, and I helped Millie clean the guest rooms where her guest had checked out, then we sat down to have lunch when Claire came by.

Claire said "Hi" to Millie and asked her how business was, and they talked a few minutes then she said, "Everyone at church today was talking about you saving Mr. Clark's life and the fire and rescue Marshal Smith said that they wanted to honor you next month for the Hero award. I'm so proud of you, there are not too many people that know CPR and if they did would probably panic. The Marshall wants to honor you at their banquet and offer free CPR and first aid classes to anyone all because of you." and Claire hugged me.

"Thank you, but I wasn't no hero, I just did what I knew to do. I thought you were talking about what happened yesterday." Ericka said.

Claire said, "What happened yesterday, I wasn't in town, I went to Luxemburg to visit an old friend that's sick."

Millie said, "Ericka rescued a little girl that found her family dead."

"Oh, my pastor at church said that they were doing funerals for two of our own, but I didn't get any details, what happened?" Claire asked and just about that time Sherry and Samantha came into the kitchen for a snack. After Millie gave them cookies, they went back to the sunroom Claire said, "I know that little girl; I've seen her sitting on her porch in a box on the steps several times."

Millie, John, and Ericka looked at each other then, Ericka said "She found her aunt and the aunt's boyfriend dead from an overdose Saturday morning. I stopped at the shop to get my sketch pad when I found her on the grass crying so I went to her house with her, and I called the police and I offered to keep the little girl until they could find relatives, but she doesn't have anyone." Ericka said.

"Oh, I'm so sorry this happened to you, but this child is lucky to have you when she needed someone." Claire said, "What will happen to her now."

"I'm trying to keep her and adopt her, she has no one and I just can't let her go into the foster care, I love this child and she needs me." Ericka said.

"If there's anything I can do just let me know, and I won't be at the shop Monday so why don't you take the day off also and we'll get back to it Tuesday." Claire said.

"Ok, thanks, I'll see you Tuesday then." Ericka said, and Claire left.

Millie asked if I wanted to go into town shopping to get Samantha some clothes. John offered to keep both girls and I asked Samantha if she wanted to go or stay and play with Sherry, so she picked Sherry, so we went shopping. We went to Walmart, and I bought under cloths pajamas and shorts tops and a couple of dresses then I called John and asked him if he could tell what size those shoes were, they she was wearing he looked and said six, so I bought her tennis shoes, sandals and a doll and a few toys.

Then we stopped at Pizza Hut and got pizza for dinner. When we got back Sherry, Samantha was asleep on the couch and John was asleep in the recliner. I couldn't help but take pictures of him asleep. He was so handsome and if everything goes south then at least I'll have a picture of him. I snapped a few pictures of Sherry and Samantha then I went back to the kitchen to help Millie. We sat out the pizza and I helped throw a salad together then I went in and woke up John and the girls for dinner. Everyone likes pizza, even Samantha ate almost two slices, then they went to play.

We sat at the table and John, Millie and I were talking about filing for temporary custody for Samantha, we plan on taking Samantha to the doctor to document her bruises and scars and see if we could get her evaluated also.

Then John said, "the Judge will want you to show proof that you're able to support a child so you may want to find a place to live on your own but sense you have a job that will help."

"Maybe I had better start looking this week when will I have to go before the Judge?" Ericka asked.

"I'm filing paperwork for an emergency hearing in the morning so most likely we'll be in court by Wednesday morning." John said.

Millie said, "That's quick; you can stay here as long as you want, we can always say you work here also if you need to."

"No John right, I need to show I'm capable of living and supporting myself and a child after the doctors tomorrow, I'll check around for apartments or house to rent." Ericka said.

We decided to take Samantha to the ER first thing in the morning, John thought it might be quicker than waiting for an appointment that might not happen today. So, after John and Sherry left, I got Samantha ready for bed and she went to sleep with no problems. I sat up and figured out my money that I had saved and brought with me and the money I have because of work, then I got my machine out and worked on Mary's dress first because it was the simplest and I lost track of time, and I had her dress finished and it was going on 5 am. I laid down for a nap and dosed off and slept tell my alarm and it went off at 7:30. I was so tired but I got up and showered and dressed then I woke Samantha up and bath her and put her in a light blue Minnie mouse dress that I bought her and I help her put on her sandals brushed her hair and I noticed that she had a scar in her hair so I wanted to mention it to the ER doctor.

While I helped her get dressed, I told her that I was taking her to the doctor to have a checkup and she shook her head yes. I helped her get ready then I took her downstairs for breakfast, but Millie had fixed her blueberry pancakes and Samantha ate one and a half then John knocked on the kitchen door and he went with me to take Samantha to the ER and Millie kept Sherry. After we checked in, they called us back. I could tell by the way Samantha was holding my hand so tight that she was scared, I whispered, "Don't worry, I'll be here the whole time." Samantha smiled and she seemed to relax some.

The doctor came in and asked, "What seems to be the problem?"

I said, "Doctor, Samantha was in an unsafe environment, and I need you to check her out."

Dr. Robins said to the nurse, "Can you take Samantha to the toy room and sit with her while we talk, then you can bring her back in when I need to examine her."

The nurse smiled, said, "Yes doctor, Samantha can you come with me, I'll show you all of our toys." Samantha looked at me.

I said, "Its ok Sammy you can go with Nurse Kelly, we'll be right here when you come back."

John and I explained the situation and I showed him the pictures I took then he said, "I have a file on this child, I reported the child's mother to social services about three months ago, I would have thought that they would have removed this child from that house." Dr. Robins said.

He brought the file in and in the three years these people lived here, Samantha was in the ER 18 times for bruises, contusions, stitches, broken bones, and a concussion from falling out of a bunk bed hitting her head on the metal rails.

We were there almost five hours and then we were sent to a conference room to meet with the doctor. Her chart showed she had broken her arm, broken her leg, broken three fingers, and had broken several ribs, she had several stitches and a concussion, and each time it was reported to Phoenix social services.

After the nurse brought Sammy back, the doctor and nurse examined Sammy and they did bloodwork, x-rays, and MRI after about five hours, we got our answers. They found drugs in Sammy system, she had burn scars and some that was just a few days old, she was malnourished and underweight she was actually almost four years old, her birthday is October 2nd. The scar on her head was recent probably within a week. He had a phycologist evaluate her and they thought that she wasn't sexually abused but that she had been beaten burned and neglected and somehow had trace amounts of drugs in her system.

We explained that I was filing for temporary custody and the doctor said that he would make sure he finishes the reports by the end of the day so that they would be ready for court Wednesday morning.

We took Samantha out to lunch, and she ate her fries and a few bites of her cheeseburger then we went back to Millie's, Samantha fell asleep, so John carried her in and laid her on the couch to finish her nap. We sat with Millie and told her everything that the doctor said.

Claire called and asked if I could come to the shop to see her, she needed to talk with me, so I had Millie and John watch over Samantha and I went to the shop.

When I got there Claire was in the back of the store and I went in, and she was sitting in her old chair by her old sewing machine. I smiled, "Hi Claire is everything ok?"

Clair smiled back, "Yes, I'm fine, I wanted to talk to you about my shop. I want you to buy it from me and I haven't shown you upstairs, but it has two-bedroom apartment up there where me and mom lived when we first open up, it needs some cleaning and maybe updated but it would be prefect for you and Samantha."

"I knew you said you were going to close the shop, but you want me to buy it, are you sure?" Ericka asked.

"Yes, I'm sure, I haven't been well for some time now and today, I got my results and I have cancer." Claire said.

"Oh, Claire I'm so sorry but you don't have to sell, I'll work your shop while you have, your treatments." Ericka said.

"Thank you, Ericka, but I'm not doing treatments, you see my best friend has cancer too, she's done chemo and radiation and she just up and quit. She decided to travel and see as much as she could before it's too late so that's what we're going to do." Clair explained.

"I don't know what to say, I'll miss you, but I understand how you feel. But the thing is I don't know if I can get a loan for this shop." Ericka said.

"You don't need a loan; we'll have everything drawled up through a lawyer and you can make a monthly payment into an account that I sat up and if something happens to me then the shop is clear and free to go straight to you. I don't have anyone left but my best friend, so we're traveling together, and you have inspired me to fulfill my dream of traveling and seeing the world. Please think about it but be quick, I'm leaving on a cruise in 20 days, and I really want you to take over my dream and turn it into your dream." Claire said.

"I feel like I'm cheating you." Ericka said.

"No, you're not; you will be fulfilling my dream for my for business to continue through you. You're a visionary and I have faith in you, come on say, yes." Claire pleaded, "While you think on it let me show you the upstairs, come on follow me."

They went upstairs and it was beautiful. It had a large living room and a huge master bedroom then a nice-sized bedroom and yes it needed to be painted and cleaned but it was beautiful.

"I accepted your offer and Claire, thank you." then we hugged, "I will miss you when you're gone." Ericka said.

Claire said, "I'll be here with you in my thoughts and prayers."

Ericka hugged Claire and whispered, "Thank you."

"You're welcome, now can you get that boyfriend of you to write up the agreement?" Claire asked.

"He's not my boyfriend but yes, I'll ask John to take care of it, why don't you come over for dinner tonight and we will meet with John and iron out the details ok." Ericka said.

"Ok I'll be there, six if that's oks." Claire asked.

"Yes, six will work, I might just order pizza, if that's ok." Ericka said.

"Pizza sounds good to me, I'll see you at six." Clair said and she left.

I locked up and went back to Millie's; everyone was either watching TV or watching the girls play with toys, so I asked John and Millie to come to the kitchen. I explained what Claire wanted and why and they both were excited for me.

John got a call, and we had court Wednesday morning at 9 am and social services are coming out tomorrow to check on Samantha and file a report.

John suggested that we move to the suit so that it appears that Samantha has her own room and that maybe we need to set it up with clothes and her toys. We moved rooms and John put the cot back in the basement and we went to Shopko and bought Samantha a few more cloths and things to put in her room. Then we showed her the room, and she crawled in her bed and smiled and played with her dolls and stuff animals. Ron called and said he would be home later tonight so John told him to come to Millie's, that's where he and Sherry would be.

I ordered pizza, spaghetti, and meatballs for dinner, and it arrived at almost six o'clock. Claire showed up and while we ate, we talked, and John took notes and asked questions. Claire had a business account and a personal account with a savings account, so she decided on $500.00 monthly payments into the savings account for ten years but if the unforeseeable happens then the business, building and all contents revert totally to Ericka Mann.

After dinner we worked out all the details then Claire left to go home. There was a knock on the front door and Ron came walking in, Sherry was so excited that she squealed with delight and went running into her daddy's arms.

John hugged Ron and said, "It's about time old man, I thought you'd ran away to Fiji or something." laughing the whole time.

"Glad to be back" Ron said, "how my baby girl been?"

"She's been good as always." John said, "But she has missed you."

"Hi Ericka, how are you, I'll get to your car as soon as I can, probably tomorrow." Ron said as he noticed the little girl standing by Ericka holding her hand. He smiled and bent down, "Now who do we have here, I'm Ron, Sherry's Daddy. What's your name?"

Samantha smiled, "I'm Sammy, I don't have a daddy or mommy."

Ron smiled, "I'm sorry about that but it looks like you have some friends, and you know sometimes friends are better than family." and Samantha laughed.

Sherry said, "Come on Sammy, let's go play" and the girls ran out of the kitchen.

Millie hugged Ron and said, "It's good to see you Ron, I bet your hungry come and sit down and I'll fix you a plate."

Ron looked at Ericka and John and smiled then he winked at Millie.

Ron said, "That sounds good, now what has been going on sense I've been away?"

John told Ron about Samantha and everything that happened while Ron ate then Millie said, "Oh and one of my guests had a heart attack and Ericka did CPR and saved his life."

"Wow, I wouldn't know how to do CPR. It's a good thing that you were here." Ron said, "that's probably something I need to check on learning."

John said, "The fire dept is honoring Ericka at the annual banquet and they're going to give free classes to anybody that wants to learn so I sign you and me up already."

"You sure have your hands full, but I gave out you name and Millie's number to my cousin that's getting married next spring I hope that's ok." Ron said, "I told her I didn't know how long you'd be in town so she said she would call you next week, I hope I haven't overstepped."

"No that's fine, I'm buying the bridal shop down the street so I'm sticking around. I appreciate all the business I can get." Ericka said.

Ron said, "I'm beat, I can't wait to get in my own bed and get some real sleep, I plan on sleeping in tomorrow then I'm meeting Chelsea for lunch then work. I'll call you about your car in the afternoon."

Ericka smiled, "That's fine, whenever you get to it, I have a rental for now."

John said, "Hey Ron can I have a few minutes before you head home?"

"Sure, John lets walk out to the garden." Ron said.

The guys went outside, and I help Millie put everything away and load the dishwasher, we could hear the guys talking loudly but we didn't say a word then Ron and John walked into the back door and Ron said to Ericka, "do you have pictures that I need to see?"

"Yes, I have pictures." and Ericka pulled out her phone and showed the pictures to him. The look on his face, you could see that he was hurt and disappointed.

Ericka said, "I'm sorry, Ron."

"Don't be, I'm to blame for being stupid enough to think she was in love with me. I had better get Sherry and get home." Ron said and went in to get his daughter.

Millie said, "It will be ok, best he knew what kind of woman she was. I'm tired, goodnight." and went to bed.

After they left and Millie went to bed, John sat down at the table.

Ericka asked John, "Are you ok?" but he said, "I don't know, maybe I should have stayed out of it."

"No, you're a good friend and Ron will get over this, just give it some time." Ericka said and put her hand on John's shoulder to comfort him. John looked up and our eyes locked and you could see the hurt and worry in his eyes, but you could also see desire as he got up and turned towards me and pulled me into his arms and he kissed me gentle at first then with more passion. I had never been kissed like this as he pulled me to him, and I could feel the passion in me, the wanting and I could feel his body so close to me that I could feel his hear beat and his hard muscles flexing as we moved to get closer to each other then I hear Samantha opening the kitchen door, so I suddenly jumped away from John, my mouth felt bruised from kissing. I could see the disappointment from stopping but I smiled and asked Samantha, "Are you ready for bed?" She shook her head yes then she said, "Can I sleep in my bed?"

"Yes, if you like." Ericka said and Sammy smiled and said, "Yes I want to."

I looked at John and said, "I need to get Sam in bed, do you want to wait?"

"No, I had better get home also, I have paperwork to draw up, but I'll call you in the morning." John said and left.

Ericka took Sam to her room and helped her get into her pajamas then tucked her in bed. She asked me to read her a story, so I read the three little pigs, and she was asleep before I got through half of the book. I kissed her on her forehead and whispered "goodnight" then I got ready for bed. I kept thinking about that kiss and where it could have gone if it wasn't for Sam walking in.

As much as I want John, I can't get involved with him but when I went to sleep, he invaded my dreams all night.

I got up early, showered and dressed then I worked on sketches and made a list of things that I needed to order when I got to the shop, Sam woke up, so I took her to the kitchen and fixed her cereal and Millie came in looking rough. "Millie, are you ok?"

Millie smiled, "I just have a headache; I'll be ok after I have coffee."

"I'll call Claire and tell her I'm not coming in today so I can be here for you." Ericka said.

"Nonsense you go to work, I'll watch Sam and Sherry coming at lunchtime. I'll be fine, I don't have any guests coming tell the weekend, so I'll just take it easy. I promise now to scoot before you're late." Millie said.

"Ok but I'll come check on you later." Ericka said and went to the shop. Claire was already there and there was four young men there having coffee with her.

Claire said, "Ericka, I want you to meet Shawn, Tom, Gary and Dave, they're here to help clear the upstairs and help us get everything in order."

Ericka said, "Hi guys, it's nice to meet you, thanks for helping, we can get started whenever you want to."

We worked upstairs all day, we carried out furniture and boxes of cloths and linens that were stained and dry rotting. Claire had ordered a dumpster and it arrived around ten so by the end of day it was almost full. Claire kept very little from upstairs so after we got it empty, I told everyone to take a late break and I went and checked on Millie.

When I walked in Chelsea was there screaming at Millie, talking about her and she was a stupid old woman that didn't know day from night.

Ericka jumped in and told Chelsea, "Get out, you have no right to be here causing trouble, if you could keep your lies straight then you wouldn't be in such a mess."

Chelsea said, "You bitch, you had better stay out of my business and stay away from John and Ron, there not in your league. You and dumb granny here need to keep your mouths shut before I shut them for you."

Ericka slapped Chelsea hard, and she hit the floor, I looked at her with fire in my eyes and said, "Don't you ever come here again, and don't you ever talk to Millie like that again, because I can take you out bitch and don't you forget it."

Chelsea got up and grabbed her bag and ran out the door. Millie started clapping and I hugged her, "Are you ok, if I knew that bitch was here, I would have come sooner."

"Ericka, your everyone's hero, but I'm afraid she causing all kinds of trouble for John and Ron." Millie said.

"Don't worry about it Millie, they are grown men, they will work it out. Where's the girls, I hope they didn't see this." Ericka said.

"I fed them lunch then they went down for a nap, thank goodness. I wouldn't want them to hear any of this." Millie said, "I didn't know you could handle yourself so well, I wouldn't want to get on your bad side." Laughing.

"How's your headache, are you feeling better, before Chelsea showed up."

"I feel better and thank you, let me fix you a sandwich before you go back to work." Millie said and went into the kitchen, I called John and told him what transpired so that he would know what to do. He said he would go see Ron and tell him then he would check on Millie so I could go back to work. I ate my sandwich then I hugged Millie and told her to call me if she needed me then I went back to work. When I got back, Claire came in after me, then the four young men showed up again and was ready to work so we swept floors then dusted and vacuum the whole top floor then the guys went and brought in ladders, trays, drop cloths, rollers, and paint.

"Claire, you don't have to have them do all this, I can work on it in the evenings." Ericka said.

"Nonsense, you need to spend as much time with Samantha as you can. She's been through so much and even though she seems fine, she may not be fine with everything that child went through." Claire said, "And anyway these guys are from church, and they volunteered. I'm going to order them pizza and let them work and quit whenever they want. I'm going home and so are you. I'll see you tomorrow after court, come by and let me know what happened." and Claire ordered pizza and left.

Ericka went to Millie's to check on everyone and John and Ron were there, and they were rather loud, so I rushed in to see what had happened. When they saw me, both John and Ron started clapping.

Ericka said, "What's going on?"

Ron said, "I hear that you handled Chelsea earlier. Thank you, Millie means a lot to me and John and I'm glad you were here and take up for Millie."

John smile and said, "I know I told you to hit her, if need be, but you didn't have to take me so literally, but I'm glad you were here, Millie doesn't deserve any problems because of us guys."

Millie said, "I'm going to check on the girl's, dinner ready by the way, I'll be right back." and left the room with tears in her eyes.

"I warned her if she came back, I'd take her out." Ericka laughs, "I think she knows I meant it."

Millie came back in with the girls and Sammy ran to me and hugged my legs, so I pick her up and hugged her, "How was your day, did you have fun?"

Sammy shook her head yes and whispered, "Millie was crying today, we gave her hugs and she said she was better."

"Thank you, I know your hugs are great and they always make me better when I'm sad." I whispered back to Sammy then I said, "Let eat, I'm starving."

Dinner was great, everyone ate and joked about Chelsea then Ericka volunteered to clean up and told Millie to go watch TV with the boys and I'd join them shortly. Ericka did the dishes and cleaned the kitchen then heard a noise outside in the backyard, so she opened the door and stepped out then suddenly something hit her, and she fell into darkness.

Ericka could feel a cold rag on her face and open her eyes as John said, "Don't move the ambulance is on the way."

Ericka tried to get up but was dizzy, so she sat back down and said, "I'm fine, I just need a minute what happened?"

"Chelsea boyfriend, we think hit you with a beer bottle." John said, "The police is here, and they met Chelsea and her boyfriend pulling out of our road, so there looking for them, I hear the ambulance."

Ron said, "I'll go and lead them in here."

"Is Millie, ok?" Ericka asked.

"She's shaken up and worried about you, but I ask her to sit with the girls, so they won't get frighten." John said.

"Sammy said Millie was crying earlier today and that she and Sherry gave her a hug and made her feel better. I was wondering if Chelsea came back after I left." Ericka said.

"I'll talk to her after we get you to the hospital." John said.

"I'm perfectly fine, I'm not going to the hospital." Ericka said as the EMS came into the kitchen.

John moved so that they could check me out the cut wasn't deep enough for stitches, but they said that I needed to stay awake for the next several hours, so after they bandaged me up and left. The girls were scared but they were glad to see me, both Sammy and Sherry hugged me and gave me kisses. Millie looked worried but I told her I was fine and hugged her and told her to go on to bed that I'd be fine, I'll probably work on my sketches and designs. John announced that he was staying the night to make sure I was ok so I worked at the table and Sammy fell asleep by him after Ron and Sherry left, so I check on them about an hour later and they both was fast asleep so I put a blanket over both of them and fixed me a cup of hot tea and worked until two am. John and Sammy were still asleep so I crawled into the recliner and went to sleep.

Millie woke me at seven, so I got up and showered and dressed in a navy dress with a white sweater and navy sandals then I woke John up and he ask, "How are you feeling?"

"Like a train hit me but I'm good for court." Ericka said.

John showered and changed into a dark grey suit and light blue shirt with a blue and white tie. Sammy woke up so I helped her with her breakfast and Millie said that she would help her with her bath and to get dressed.

Ericka gave Millie a hug and then she hugged Samantha and whispered, "I love you, I'll be back."

Samantha hugged me and said, "I love you" and I almost cried.

We drove to court in silence and when we got there, John went to check in and I sat out on a bench in the hallway with several other people that were there for family court. They called Samantha's name, and I went into a little room and John and the district attorney were there and the Lady from Social Services and the Police chief were there also. Everyone was talking to John and each other but me and finally I asked. "What's going on, is there a problem."

The district attorney said, "Ms. Mann are you willing to take on a problem child and raise her with knowing she's been abused and neglected and has had drugs in her system. We don't know what all she's been through. You could have serious problems with her later on, we just don't know."

"Yes, I want her, and I am willing to raise her and protect her and if she needs doctors or extra help in school, I can handle it. I'm not afraid, I love this child," Ericka said.

Mrs. Carter from Social services asked, "We just worry that maybe it will be too much, and you don't have any support, no family, and no job. You're not even a resident here."

"I have a business and a place to live, its being painted as we speak. I bought the bridal shop, and it has an apartment upstairs for us to live in and we'll be moving within two weeks. I have support of my friends and I have several letters of recommendations from them." Ericka said.

John said, "I see no reason why you wouldn't agree to let Ericka Mann have custody of Samantha Jones, she has a business and housing, friends that's willing to help her if she needs it, she has transportation, and she's truly cares about this child."

The district attorney said, "Ok let's get out there and let the Judge make his decision, he's the one to make it official one way or another."

We went into the court room, and we went up front and sat down until the clerk called our names then we went up before Judge Harrison. The Court Clerk read the case number and details then read the motion to give me temporary custody.

Judge Harrison said, "Ms. Mann, after reading all the information, I know you have no family, no friends, and no support, also you don't even reside here, your last address was in Louisville Kentucky, so I'm not sure I'm comfortable giving you a child that will undoubtedly have emotion problems."

"Judge, I have faith and enough love to get this little girl through all the good and bad times that are coming her way. I lived in the system growing up; I was sent to one foster home then to another. I was treated like a slave most of the time and I don't want that for Samantha, she needs me, and I honestly need her, I love her as if she was mine. If you give me temporary custody today, then I'll prove to you that you made the right decision when we come back to court. I just bought a bridal business with an apartment. I have transportation and I have several friends here and I want to make this town my home." Ericka said.

John said, "Judge we have letters from several friends of Ms. Mann since she has been here, and she has bought a bridal shop business and will be moving into the apartment above the store next week. She has several dress orders, and her business will only increase with the talent she has."

"I see you have been doing your homework, Ms. Mann." the Judge said, "I'll read over the documents and make my decision. We'll recess for 15 minutes" and bang his gable.

John smiled nervously and said, "I think it will go in your favor, think positive."

Ericka said, "I don't know, I have no roots anywhere and he knows that."

Judge Harrison came back in, and the court clerk said, "All Rise."

Judge Harrison smiled, "Alright, I have read all letters and documentation, I give you temporary custody, but I'll have social services keep tabs on you and make monthly visits then we'll revisit this hearing in six months, Congratulations."

Then the Judge picks up his garble and bangs it "next case" the Judge said.

Ericka squealed, "Yes, thank you" jumped up and ran into John arms and hugged him and kissed him. He returned her kiss and then he pulled back and said, "We had better get to Millie's and give Samantha the good news."

"Ok yes let's go, I can't wait to tell everyone the news, but first I have to go to the bathroom. I'll meet you in the hallway in a few minutes." Ericka said.

"Ok, you go ahead, and I'll be out in a few minutes, I want to talk to the district attorney." John said.

After Ericka left the court room John asked Robert Stevens the district attorney if they had any details about Samantha's life but he said they found a grandmother but she's in a nursing home with Alzheimer's so he saw no reason why Ericka would lose her probably when they come back to court, she could ask to adopt her and mostly the Judge will most likely agree. John called Millie and told her the good news then he went out in the hallway to wait for Ericka.

John and Ericka went to Millie's and when they got there, they walked in and everyone yelled, "Congratulations" Claire, Ron, Sherry, Mary, Lucy, and Sarah were there along with a few friends, I've met through Millie and John.

Every hugged and had encouraging words and offered any help that I might need, I excused myself and went to find Samantha. She was playing with Sherry and Bobby a little boy that was Lucy nephew.

Ericka said, "Samantha, can you come here, I want to tell you something."

Samantha said, "Are you giving me away?" in a sad voice.

"No honey, the Judge said that I could keep you if that's ok with you?" Ericka said, praying that this is what Samantha wants.

"Oh yes I want to stay with you." Samantha said smiling and threw herself in Ericka's lap hugging her, and then she pulled back, "Will you be my mommy?"

"Yes, I'll be your mommy and I'll treat you like a princess because I love you and you are my princess." Ericka said almost in tears.

"Yeah, I have a mommy, can you be Sherry's mommy, she wants a mommy too?" Samantha said.

Ericka smiled, "I'll see what I can do." and she gave her a hug and kisses "Now go play and have fun."

The party was great everyone stayed late and after everyone left but John Ron and Sherry, while the girls played, we sat at the table with Millie, and I told everyone what Samantha said and how excited she was to have a mommy then I told them that she asked me to find Sherry a mommy because she wants one too.

Ron said, "The way I'm going with women, Sherry will never have a mother."

Millie said, "Maybe you're not looking in the right place."

Ron said, "Well if there's a store to buy one, send me the address." he said laughing.

"You know what I mean, why you don't start going to church, Sherry loves it when me or Lucy takes her. You need to meet people and become their friend before you fall in love." Millie said.

"Church isn't my thing, you know how I feel, if there was a god, then why did he abandon me and John when we were little?" Ron said.

"He didn't abandon us, our parents did, and we suffered because of it, but you have to let go of that anger Ron, it's not healthy to be so resentful." John said.

"It's the same thing." Ron said, "Hell the only thing good that happened to us was Millie and Joe."

Millie smiled, "Ron do you remember going to church with us, then Joe would take you boys fishing afterwards. Maybe that was God's plan sense we couldn't have children, he gave us you two boys. I'll always be grateful for having you boys in my life, me and Joe loved you as if you were our very own sons, we couldn't have asked for anything better." Millie said with tears in her eyes.

Ron said, "I love you Millie, you were the best mom a boy could have. I know we weren't always good, but you and Joe was always there for us."

John said, "He's right Millie, you and Joe loved us like we were your own and we love you back just like you and Joe were our real parents. I just wish Joe was still with us, I miss him always leading us in the right direction."

Millie smiled, "He's in heaven watching over us all. Now I need to clean up these dishes, so everyone scatters."

Ericka said, "No Millie, you take it easy me and these two guys will help me clean up the kitchen you go rest and relax and we'll join you when we're done, now you scoot, come on boys let's get busy."

Millie joined the girls in watching TV and after Ericka, John and Ron finished with the kitchen they joined her and watched the news.

Ron gave Millie a hug and said, "I'm taking Sherry home and getting her ready for bed, Lucy watching Sherry the next couple of days, so I'll see you later this week, if you need me just call. And Congratulations again Ericka on getting custody of Sammy, she's a lucky girl."

Ericka said, "Thank you but I'm the lucky one."

After Ron and Sherry left John said it was time to get home and asked Ericka "Would you walk out with me?"

"Of course, Millie I'll be right back." Ericka said as she walked outside onto the porch with John.

John caught her hand and pulled her to him, "I've wanted to do this all day" and he kissed her and pulled her into his arms, and they kiss instantly sent a fire through Ericka and she just melted into his arms. It was like they were one instead of two people and as the long kiss and embraced ended John said, "I'm sorry, I got carried away."

Ericka looked up at him with wanting in her eyes, "I think we both did, I have never been kissed like that. If we keep this up I afraid of what might happen."

John smiled, "I'd never hurt you, you know that don't you?"

"Yes, I know but I've had such a messed-up life, I wouldn't want you to get hurt. I don't believe in love and happiness that's for children, and I don't believe in fairy tales."

"You're afraid of love and I understand it. I don't know if I will believe in happiness ever after, but I have never felt this way about anyone, you fill my thoughts day and night. I think I'm falling in love with you Ericka Mann and I want to take you out for a date and really get to know you and give you a chance to get to know me. Will you go out with me Friday night to dinner?" John asked smiling.

Ericka smiled and said, "Yes I'd love to go out with you Friday night."

John said, "Great I'll pick you up at 6:30, I can't wait tell then." and he kissed her and whispered, "Goodnight" and down the steps to his car and Ericka stood there watching until his taillights disappeared then went in and told Millie night and took Samantha up to get ready for bed. Ericka slept great that night, she dreamed of John and the way he kissed her. The next morning Ericka got up humming happily, showered, dressed, and had her coffee while Samantha ate breakfast then she kissed her daughter goodbye and went to the shop to work.

Ericka thought I never thought my life could be this great, but I have a great life. I have friends I just bought a business and home and I get to raise this adorable child that I love so much plus I have John who's really interested in me. If this is a dream I sure don't want to wake up. The sun was shining, it was a beautiful day, so Ericka walked to the shop, but when she got there the police were there with Clair, someone had vandalized the shop. The front door someone threw a brick through it then they sprayed paint all over the front doors and the big picture window. I ran over to where Clair and the chief of police James were standing "Are you ok Claire?"

Clair said, "Yes, it was this way when I got here but whoever threw the brick through the glass door left a message for you."

"For me, who do I know that would cause this much trouble because of me. I haven't been here long enough to make anyone that mad." Ericka said.

James said, "The note said, "I told you to keep your distance and stay out of my life." Do you know anyone that doesn't like you or anyone that's threatening you sense you got here?"

"No, the only person I've had trouble with was Chelsea, Ron's supposed girlfriend. I caught her yelling at Millie and calling her names, so I put her in her place and told her to get out and not come back." Samantha said.

James said, "Do you know her last name?"

"No but Ron or John would know, the other night I got knocked out with a beer bottle and they think Chelsea X-boyfriend hit me." Ericka said.

After the police left, I called John and told him what happened then I asked Clair who I could call to get the glass repaired in the door and she said she had already called, and they were on their way. I got glass cleaner a scraper and newspaper and cleaned the paint of the big picture window and about 8 men from Clair's church showed up and repaired the door, one of the men did alarms, so he installed on one each door and windows by the end of the day the window and door was back to normal, and the men got most of the paint off the brick and siding. I ordered pizza and fed everyone and by 5:00 o'clock I was tired, so I walked home slowly and when I got to Millie's house there was several people there arguing in the front yard, it was Chelsea two men I didn't recognized and Chelsea X-boyfriend. I dialed John's number and when he answered I told him to "Call the police Chelsea and three men are here auguring with Millie." and hung up.

Ericka walked over and asked, "What was going on?"

Chelsea said, "It's none of your business, I'm here to make granny understand that she needs to watch her mouth or face the consequences."

Ericka said, "I'm telling you all to get off the property the police is on the way and if you don't move your ass then I'll move it for you, understand Bitch."

Chelsea X-boyfriend said, "Don't talk to her like that or next time I'll gut you instead of hitting you with a bottle."

I reached behind me and pulled out my pocketknife just in case I need it before the police came, then I told Millie, "Go inside, I'll be there in a minute." then I turned to Chelsea and said, "I've had it with you and your crazy men, now get off the property now!"

Chelsea said, "I don't have to listen to you, you're nothing but trash." and walked up close to me and whispered, "Johnny boy wants to rip you to pieces and show you what a real man is like. The last woman I sent him after could barely walk or talk and I stood there watch the whole thing and when he got done with her, I didn't even have to hold her down while he took his pleasure on her so if you know what's good for you get out of my face and my business."

Johnny boy said, "I'll rip your clothes off and have my friends hold you down and I'll show you what a man can do." as he got so close to me that I could almost feel the heat off him then he put his hand on my rear and I jumped and pulled out my knife, I heard the sirens and Johnny grabbed me by the hand causing me to drop my knife and they took off with Johnny dragging me through the yard. I was screaming and yelling for help and Millie came out the back door with a shot gun and shot it in the air and everyone stopped dead in their tracks.

I jerked my arm loose and ran toward Millie as the police pulled up and got out surrounding Chelsea, Johnny and the other two men. John and Ron both showed up and within a few minutes of the police.

Chelsea, Johnny and the two men were arrested and put in the police cars and the detective and chief took statements and they also searched their car and found rope, chloroform, a doll, little girl cloths and a ransom note for Ron and John, they also found drugs, loaded guns and knives in the car also.

The police said it looked like a kidnapping scheme and that we we're lucky. After the police left, Ron went to get Sherry and when he returned, he suggested that we all go out to dinner, so everyone got ready, and we all went to Randy's Steak House. The girls were great, and the food and company were fantastic. Ron paid for the dinner, so John left a big tip for the waitress then after saying goodbye to Ron and Sherry in the parking lot, we went back to Millie's.

Samantha was asleep so John carried her up to her bed and Millie said Goodnight then it was just me and John alone in the kitchen. Ericka was nervous and her heart was racing, you could feel the electricity in the room. John walked over to Ericka and pulled her into his arms and lowered his head and kissed Ericka on the lips gently at first but then it deepened into a more sensual and passionate kiss causing Ericka legs to almost buckle under her she had never been kissed like this. She could feel the urge to want more, and she felt like she needed him and as she responded to him the slide his arms up and under her blouse and over her breast, Ericka felt the tingle sensation as his hand brushed across her nipple and she wanted more. John hand slide to her back and unhook her bra and then his moved his hand to touch her breast, he coupled them, tweeting her nipple and making her feel hot and wet between her legs. John pulled back and looked Ericka in her eyes and whispered "I want you" and Ericka said "Yes I want you to" and John pick Ericka up and carried her to her room and laid her on the bed then he went over and shut the door where Samantha was sleeping then he walked over to the bed and laid down almost on top of Ericka and kissed her again and again, then he raised her blouse and lick her nipple and Ericka groaned and then he suckled it and while he squeezed the other breast and nipple Ericka wasn't sure of what was happening to her but she squealed in pleasure. John took his mouth off her nipple and kissed her on the mouth deeply then he slid her blouse and bra off completely and he stood up and took his shirt off and reached down and pulled her shirt off and slid her black lacy underwear off and Ericka sat up and reached for Johns belt she undid this belt and unbutton and unzipped her pants and slid them down and John step out of his cloths Ericka could see how swollen he was and reached for his boxers and slide them down looking shocked, she had seen little boys naked when changing diapers or helping them potty train but she had never seen a man naked before.

    She reached out and touched him and John groaned in pleasure then he pushed her back and he kissed her nipples and ran his hand between her legs and felt her wetness then he slid down and buried his head between her legs and she groaned and moaned in pure ecstasy until her body couldn't take it any longer then John lifted himself up and on to her as he entered her, causing her body to convulsed with pleasure until they both were exhausted. They fell asleep in each other's arms and when morning came and Ericka woke, she laid there watching John sleep he was so handsome and if there was a real love then this would be prefect but knowing from experience that love is just a myth, and it causes pain and suffering and such heart break that it's not worth having. Ericka felt sad to have this beautiful night with John, but she knew that it could never happen again her life needs to be concentrating on making Samantha's life happy and healthy and that didn't consist of having a man in it to cause unhappiness.

Maybe she and John can remain friends but, in most cases, men don't want just a friendship they wanted a relationship that includes anything that they want and nothing of what a woman wants but then her mother took her dad's side, and they took drugs over me so that doesn't say much about most women either.

Ericka smooth hair out of Johns face and his eyes open at the touch of her hands and he turned and kissed her "Morning beautiful" John said with a twinkling in his eyes.

"Morning to you too, it's almost eight we'd better get up and dressed before Samantha wakes up." Ericka said.

"Oh, if we have too." John said, "Why don't we take Sam out today, we can go to the zoo or the children museum. I bet she's never been to either what do you think?"

"I have work to do today, I'm supposed to meet with Claire at 10 to go over the papers then I'll bring them to you after lunch." Ericka said, "we'll have to do the zoo another day, Ok."

"Alright if you insist, I'll get dressed and if you want to wake Sam up, I'll take her down to breakfast while you shower and dress." John offered.

"Ok great, I'll go get Samantha up and dressed and you get dressed." Ericka said and went into Samantha's room.

Samantha was awake lying there with tears in her eyes; Ericka sat down on the bed and asked, "What's the matter Samantha?"

"I came into your room to tell you I had a bad dream, but you were with Uncle John, are you sending me away?" Samantha asked as she started crying.

"No of course not, I just got you honey, and I'll never send you away. Why would you even think that?" Ericka asked as she pulled Samantha into her arms. Samantha said, "Mommy said I was bad because her friend liked me, so I had to sleep in a box and stay in the closet when he was there."

"We'll you don't have to sleep in a box or closet ever again, you are my princess and I love you. I just want to make you happy, I wish I could take all those nightmares away, but it will get better I promise." Ericka said and hugged her.

"I love you mommy and I love Uncle John." Samantha said in a light voice.

John said, "I love you too pumpkin, are you hungry, let's go get breakfast." Sam jumped up, "ok" and went running to him and he caught her and swung her around and hugged her and kissed her on her cheek.

"I'll have Millie bath and dress her after she eats ok." John said, "You had better get ready it's getting late."

"Ok thanks I'll be down in a few minutes." Ericka said and rushed into the shower.

After getting dressed in jeans and t-shirt she hurried down in time to see Millie and kiss Samantha on her forehead "I'll be back later today, call me if you need anything Millie." and out the door Ericka went.

Claire was already at the shop when Ericka arrived, Father Morris was there at Claire's church and Claire introduced them and explained that Father Morris wanted to personally invite me to the award ceremony next week.

Father Morris said, "It's so nice to meet you, I have heard such good things about you, and I'll be at the fireman and policeman's annual dinner and awards ceremony, and they have nominated you for the Hero Award which is next Friday evening. You will have a table of eight so you can bring up to seven guests with you and it's a formal affair, black tie, and all that. Do you have any questions?"

"No, I'm honored but I wasn't a hero, I just did what I was taught, and anyone would have done the same as me." Ericka said.

"You may not see how special you are, but a lot of people see you as their hero. I'll be there and if you need anything just ask, Goodbye." Father Morris said and left.

Claire said, "He really likes you, now I'm going to get us coffee and scones, you sit down and start reading those papers I've already read them so now it's your turn."

Ericka read through all the papers and when Claire came back in, we signed them, and she gave them to me to take to John. Then we went through everything in the office and Claire showed me everything throughout the building then she took me to the bank and introduced me to Mr. Collins the bank manager and he had heard the story of the CPR and was as nice as he could be. Claire switched the business account into my name, then she switched her saving account to where I would make the monthly deposit and then she took me to her safety deposit box and open it and there was a silver baby spoon, a baby ring, baby bracelet and a miniature silver mirror, brush, and comb that she took out and gave me.

"I can't take that Claire, you need to give it to someone in your family." Ericka said.

"I have no family left and I was once pregnant and me and my husband bought this for our baby but sadly to say it wasn't meant to be and it's been here all this time along with a 100 savings bond so I would like you to have them for Samantha, you can always tell her there from Aunti Claire." Claire said laughing.

"Thank you, Claire, I'll take good care of them I promise." Ericka said after we got done at the bank, we went to lunch at Waldorf's deli and as we sat there John came in with Chelsea and they sat in the back corner talking and they looked cozy, I could hear Chelsea laughing and calling John darling and even though they sat across from each other Chelsea kept leaning over the table showing her low-cut neckline giving John a full view of her breast.

I couldn't stand it any longer I told Claire it was time to leave and get back to the shop, so they left and went back to the bridal shop and all of the fabric and sewing notions had arrived, so I got busy and started sewing and working on my designs.

I did Sarah's Dress first and I worked tell six o'clock. I figured that since it was Friday that I might come and work some this weekend after I shop for furniture and household goods I could unload at the shop and work through the afternoon. I think I'll bring Sam with me so she can see her room, I'm hoping to get to move next weekend if the weathers good. Claire left at four, so I locked up and went to Millie's. When I got there, I apologized to Millie for being so late then, but she said it was fine, Ron and Sherry were there visiting and John coming to dinner also, so I had plenty of time.

Ericka thought maybe he'll explain what he was doing with Chelsea. But when John arrived, he smiled and said "Hi" and I gave him the papers that me and Claire signed then during dinner, I told everyone about the award dinner next Friday.

Millie said, "Oh my gosh that's great, George and Nancy are coming in next Wednesday and staying tell the following Wednesday. They wanted to thank you dear."

"That's prefect, I can take seven guests with me, so I want you all to go with me and George and Nancy" Ericka said.

"Their daughter Amanda coming with them do you have an extra seat for her?" Millie asked.

"Yes, I have seven, so you, Ron, John and Claire make four and George, Nancy and Amanda will make seven that worked out perfectly, I just have to find a babysitter." Ericka said.

"I'll ask Lucy, she usual takes care of Sherry when I'm out on Fridays so I'll call her and ask ok." Ron said.

"Thank you, Ron, let me know." Ericka said.

After the girls left the table, I ask John, "How was your day?"

"It was ok, nothing important going on." John said.

"Have you heard when Chelsea and her men are going to court, I'd like to be there." Ericka said.

"You don't have to go, if I hear anything, I'll tell you but the saying no news is good news." John said nervously and changed the subject to Ron and my car then I helped Millie clear the dishes and I washed and put away the pots and pans while the dishwasher was running.

Millie asked, "What's bothering you, Ericka?"

"John is, he's lying, I saw him at the deli with Chelsea today she's already out of jail and he's lying all about it. I know I have problems trusting but if he can't tell me the truth then I'm right, I can't trust him and without trust there nothing between us." Ericka said sadly.

"Maybe he has a reason." Millie said, "Why don't you just come out and ask him?"

Ericka said, "Because I shouldn't have to ask him why he's lying. I really don't care, now that the dishes are done, I'm going to go upstairs to work. I'll come get Samantha when Sherry leaves." and Ericka went upstairs with tears running down her face. After she got to her room, she scolded herself for following for John, she knew better but her heart didn't. She worked on dresses and John brought Sam up, I had forgotten the time as usual when working. Sam went to her room to play, and John walked over to me and put his arms around my shoulders and hugged me, "I missed you, maybe when you get moved, we can revisit what happened the other night."

"Hardly, I told you I don't believe in fairy tales. I have a business to run and a child to raise and I don't have time for you or anyone else in my life." Ericka said.

"I thought you enjoyed the other night, I thought we were getting close." John said.

"My life revolved around my child and my career nothing else, now if you'll excuse me, I have worked to do." Ericka said.

"Why are you mad at me, what did I do?" John asked.

"Nothing, I just have my priorities straight now if you don't mind, I'm busy." Ericka said.

"Fine, if that's what you want." John said and slammed the door as he left.

Ericka couldn't work anymore, she helped Sam get a bath and, in her pajamas, and into bed then she slipped on her nightgown and crawled into bed and cried herself to sleep.

Ericka woke with a headache and got ready to go shopping. Millie was keeping Sam today so that Ericka could go buy furniture for the apartment. She went to Carter Furniture and Décor and found a white princess bedroom suite for Sam, a sea blue bedroom set with the queen bed, dresser, nightstands, chest, and vanity then she bought a living room suite and end tables and a small dining room table with four chairs and hutch. It was really fun picking out furniture for the first time ever. Then she went shopping at Meller's for bedding and towels and household goods and after she checked out, one of the boys offered to help her load her car.

As they were loading the back of her car, Chelsea walked up and said, "I see your leaving, it's about time. I told you that you weren't in John's lead. John likes classy women not damsel in distress no matter how trashy you are, you have no class."

After the night I had, I just couldn't take it any longer. I turned and slugged Chelsea in the face and she went flying onto the blacktop. Charlie the boy helping load the car eyes got big and he said, "good one, mam." Chelsea turned and her nose and mouth was bleeding and she said "You bitch, I'll have you and that old bag gang raped repeatedly and then slowly tortured tell you both die." and before she could say another word, Ericka hit her again and again and there was several people that pulled her off Chelsea, the police was called and showed and the EMS came and took Chelsea, they said she had a broken nose and her front tooth was knocked out, and I didn't have a scratch on me.

James showed up and Chelsea said, I attacked her for no reason, she was just going grocery shopping so after the ambulance left James asked me, "What really happened.?" I told him what happened and what was said, and he asked if there were any witnesses. A young woman said, "I heard her say she would have her gang raped."

Charlie the boy that help me load my car said, "She threaten an old lady also and that she would have them tortured until they died." The police took their statements and let me leave but James advised me to call John.

"I will James and thank you." Ericka said.

I drove to Millie's and John was already there waiting for me. I walked in and Millie asked what happened and why was I covered in blood which I never noticed that I had Chelsea blood on me. "It's nothing I'm going to change clothes" and went upstairs and John followed me and when I got in my room, John said, "Ericka we need to talk."

Ericka said looking at John, "It's too late to talk now; none of this would have happened if you would have been honest with me."

"I was working with the police, I couldn't say anything, if I had known she would have come after you, I would have said something." John said, "But clearly you can take care of yourself, the hospital said Chelsea had a broken nose, a concussion and missing teeth, you did a good job on her."

"Well, it's too late now, just go and if I go to jail and Samantha loses the only stable life, she's ever had then it's you to blame, now get out." Ericka said and took off her shirt and jeans and changed into clean ones. Then she looked at John and said, "Get out and don't bother me again." and John walked out, and Ericka threw herself on the bed and cried.

John could hear Ericka crying and knew it wasn't him that she needed, so he went and told Millie everything, hoping that Millie could help Ericka understand. But Millie was mad, "You know Chelsea was gunning for Ericka all along and all you did was allow her to go after Ericka and you didn't even warn anyone of us about her being out of jail but let me tell you, Ericka knew she saw you and Chelsea at the deli, and she asked you about Chelsea at dinner and you lied to her. You brought this on yourself, and you need to fix it."

The look of disappointment in Millie broke John heart, but she's right. I didn't handle this right John thought and left and went to see James to see what if anything would happen because of him.

James said, "Nothing going to happen to Ericka, there was witnesses that heard Chelsea threaten Ericka and Millie and as far as I'm concern that bitch can rot in hell after what she said." James handed John the statements and John was furious and wanted to kill Chelsea himself, but James said that the DA agreed that Chelsea over played her hand and that she was going away for a long time. Then the phone rang, James answered it and went pale he turned to John and said, "Come on, that bitch just escape from the hospital."

John said, "She's headed to Millie's."

James radio for help to go to Millie's place and John called Ron at his shop but he didn't answer. They pulled up to Millie's, and they saw Millie and Sam standing out on the sidewalk with two patrol cars that had just arrived. They hopped out and Millie said Ericka was keeping Chelsea occupied while they escaped, and something happened to Ron, but she didn't know what.

Ericka came down and Millie had fixed her something to eat and Millie asked her "Do you want to talk about what happened?"

"No not really but you need to know what happened." Ericka said.

"I don't need to know if you don't want to tell me." Millie insisted.

"When Chelsea threatens me, she also threatens you Millie and I just lost it. I can take care of myself but when she threatens you, I think I would have killed her if I wasn't pulled off of her today. You mean the world to me, and I don't ever want someone to hurt you and I believe Chelsea would do exactly what she said she'd do." Ericka said with tears running down her cheeks Millie got up and hugged her.

"You mean the world to me too, I have never had a girl before but I'm proud of you as if you're my daughter. Now eat and quit crying before Sam come in." Millie said.

Ericka ate and Sam came in and they all had ice cream and then the door flew open, and it was Ron, "Are you too ok, I just heard the news, you need to lock up every window and door, now."

Millie said, "What's got in you, it's still daylight, I don't lock up tell dark."

"Don't you know Chelsea escaped the hospital about an hour ago? Millie where's Joe's 38, I was in such a hurry I forgot to grab mine from the shop." Ron said.

"It's in my bedroom top draw nightstand." Millie said, as everyone hurrying to lock all the windows and doors.

Ron ran to Millie's bedroom to get her handgun and then we heard a loud thump down the hallway, Ericka told Millie to stay with Sam as she went down the hallway toward Millie's bedroom, "Ron are you ok, what was that sound?"

As she got almost to Millie's bedroom door Chelsea steps out in the hallway, "Hello Ericka bet you didn't expect to see me again so soon?"

"What did you do to Ron?" Ericka demanded.

"Don't worry about Ron, he'll live but I can't say the same for you and granny." Chelsea said nastily, "You two have caused me enough trouble, I'm going to enjoy killing you two."

"Chelsea why are you such a bitch, don't you think I can handle myself where your concern, you look like hell by the way, thanks to me." Ericka said she was hoping Millie and Sam would get out and go for help.

"I'm going to enjoy killing you in front of that precious little girl then after I'm done with you two, I'll kill that little girl you saved, by shooting her in the head right between her little eyes," Chelsea said.

Ericka thought it's now or never Ericka dived into one of the guest rooms, "Come and get me Chelsea."

Chelsea said, "You bitch, I'll get you." and as she came down the hallway to enter the room Ericka tackled her and they fought for the gun, and it went flying into the hallway and Chelsea tried to get free and Ericka threw her over the cedar chest and jumped on her hitting her again and again until someone was pulling her off Chelsea.

John tried to call Ron at his shop, but he didn't answer. They pulled up to Millie's, and they saw Millie and Sam standing out on the sidewalk with two patrol cars. They hopped out and Millie said Ericka was keeping Chelsea occupied while they escaped, and something happened to Ron, but she didn't know what. James and John went into thru the kitchen with the other officers behind them they could hear the fight in the guest room, so James sent one officer to check on Ron and he and John and the other officer went into the guest room Ericka was on top of Chelsea beating the tar out of her. James and John grab hold of Ericka and John pulled her into his arms, "It's ok, we are here your safe."

It was John and James that pulled me off Chelsea. I was covered in blood from Chelsea, and I thought Chelsea was dead, she wasn't moving so I turned, and John grabs hold of Ericka and drags her off Chelsea and hugged her relieved to find her winning as usual. Pulled me into his arms, James came around us, to check on Chelsea. Ericka looked up with relief and turned into John.

Suddenly I felt a sharp stinging pain and I could feel darkness surrounding me as I looked shocked and fainted. James came around to John and Ericka just in time to see Chelsea throw a knife into Ericka and James yelled to stop and shot Chelsea, but it was too late the knife went into Ericka's back.

Everything was hectic, the ambulance was here for Ron and Ericka and the coroner came for Chelsea and Millie, Sam and Lucy showed up with Sherry to check on Ron. Millie and John went to the hospital and Lucy took both girls home with her after they calmed them down. James came to the hospital, Ron had a concussion and stitches, and Ericka went into surgery and had over a hundred stitches, and they kept her overnight and released the following morning. John stayed the night with her and brought her home around noon the next day.

Ericka was sore but glad to be going home to see Millie and Sam, John was extra careful with everything he said or did, he wasn't sure if Ericka would ever forgive him. John drove slowly and careful on the way home, Ericka said, "they loaded me with pain meds so that I could get home today not next week, let's speed it up John. I'm alright just sore but I want to see Millie and Samantha to make sure they are ok."

"Ok I just didn't want to hurt you." John said.

They were silent the rest of way home, when we pulled up there was Claire, James, Ron, Sherry, and Millie standing out front. James and Ron helped Ericka out of the SUV and into the house. Millie insisted that I sit in the recliner so that the girls could sit on the arms and not hurt me. After I got settled into the recliner there was a knock at the door, and it was Father Morris and the guys that helped us clean and paint the apartment with food from the parish. He said a prayer and offered to help any way he could. Jamie and Berry offered to help me move next weekend and I told them that I had furniture coming next Saturday morning between 9 and 12 and they said they would be there, after they left the girls sat with me for a while then they got down to play, everyone talked, and I dozed off for a nap. I woke later and Ron was asleep in the overstuff chair and everyone else was probably in the kitchen. I eased out of the recliner to go to the restroom and as I started down the hallway Sherry screamed, I turned and her and Sam were standing in tears, and everyone came running. Ericka asked Sam and Sherry "What's the matter?"

Sherry said, "You have blood everywhere." and Ron and John told the girls, "It's ok, Millie will help Ericka change her dressing, she's fine." and they took the girls to the sunroom. Claire and Millie helped me change my shirt and dressing then Claire went and changed the cover on the recliner so that the girls wouldn't get upset when they saw the blood.

Millie asked, "Did the doctor say that you'd bleed like this?"

"No, but I feel fine, how does it look?" Ericka said.

Claire said, "it looks good but it's bleeding, I'll call in case they want to know."

Claire said, "The doctors said that bleeding is normal but if it gets red, painful or bleeds heavily then come back in."

We went to the kitchen and Millie fixed hot tea and scones and Ericka ate three and John came in and said, "I see you have your appetite back."

"Are you trying to say I'm a pig." Ericka asked laughing.

"No but you do eat good." John said smiling.

"I don't remember you complaining before." Ericka said.

"Who's saying I'm complaining, I think you feel just right." John said winking.

Ericka blushed, "How's Ron feeling, he was asleep when I got up to go to the bathroom?"

"The girls screaming woke him and now he has a headache, so I gave him Tylenol and a beer." John said.

Millie said, "Great combination, you two boys have no sense. I'm ordering Pizza for dinner and were going to have a peaceful evening."

Claire said, "I'm going home so everyone can rest."

"No, you stay and eat with us" Millie insisted.

"Ok, but I need to be home before dark I'm having trouble with night blindness." Claire said.

Pizza arrived and everyone was eating when the phone rang it was for Ericka, after Ericka got off the phone, she had tears on her cheeks John jumped up "Honey what's the matter?"

"That was Professor Lyons, his wife Lulu passed away Friday night. He's been trying to call me, but I guess with everything going on I didn't get his calls." Ericka said.

Claire hugged me and said, "At least she's not suffering anymore, she's like your guardian angel, if she wouldn't have sent you out here, we would not have found you."

Millie said, "Like she always told you, when one door closes another open. Death is like that too, but I know it hurts but you have all of us to help you through this."

"Thank you all but I think I'm going to bed can you help with Samantha tonight?" Ericka asked Millie.

"Of course, dear, do you want to sleep downstairs in the other guest room" Millie asked.

"No, I'm fine I'll take it easy on the stairs, I'll see you tomorrow." Ericka said as she walked out of the dining room and slowly up the stairs.

John said, "I'll go with her." but Claire said, "She needs this time alone to grieve for her friend, if she needs you, she'll let you know."

Millie said, "She's right, let her be, if she needs someone, she will let us know but for now just let her be."

John and Ron watch Lilo and Stitch with the girls and after the movie, Sam said, "Is my mommy, ok?"

John said, "Yes she's just sad she lost her friend today, but she still loves you a bunch."

Ron said, "let's make you girls a tent to sleep in tonight and me and Uncle John will sleep on the couches in case you need us."

"Yeah", the girls shouted, and Millie got them blankets and pillows and after everyone ate pizza Claire went home and the guys help the girls make their tents and then they read a story to them, and they both fell asleep, so John and Ron made their bed on each couch then Millie went to bed.

As the week went on Ericka got feeling better, she worked on the dresses and went to the shop, but she took it easy most of the time. Wednesday when she came home George and Nancy were there along with their daughter Amanda. They thanked me and insisted on taking me and Millie out to dinner, but I told them that I couldn't go and explained about Samantha, but they insisted on taking us out and that included Samantha. I was a little nervous because I haven't taken her out very often because of how everything's been going but she did fine, we went to a steak house and Sam was good as gold and ate really well and after we got back, she hugged George, Nancy and Amanda and said thank you. I excused us and I got her ready for bed and I followed suit. The next morning, I saw Millie for a few minutes and then headed to work. Then it dawned on me it was Thursday and Ericka realized she didn't have anything to wear Friday night to the award dinner. Claire said that we could go through all the dresses at the shop and maybe find something, so we spent the whole afternoon going through boxes and bags of dresses that had never been unpacked then we found a black box that had never been opened and as we open the box there was this beautiful long black dress. Clair said it was prefect and insisted that I try it on, it fit perfectly as we put it back on the hanger I saw the designer tag and it was a Lulu dress and she remember learning about different designers in college and Lulu was a designer that made beautiful designs then disappeared from the world of design and as she looked at how the dress was made it had all her stitches that she herself used then it hit her like a ton of bricks, Lulu was her friend Lulu Lyons the professor wife that taught her to sew and mentored her. She told Claire all about her and Claire said that the small back room that we hadn't touched yet was full of black box company. We decided to do that another day, so Claire helped me pick out Black heels and a small black handbag then after we got everything pick out Claire insisted on taking me home to rest before dinner so after I got home, I hung up the dress and then I called Professor Lyons to see how he was doing. We talked for over an hour, and he told me that Lulu wanted me to have something special of her's and that he sent it earlier in the week. It should be there any time this week, he thought maybe today or tomorrow. He said he plans on coming out to see me sometime this fall and make sure that I can use Lulu's sewing things. I thank him so much for letting me be part of her life. After I got off the phone, I laid down for a nap and when I woke up Millie said she had a surprise for me. So, I went downstairs, and she told me to go outside, so as I opened the front door there was a moving truck parked out front.

"Millie, I don't see anything except a truck parked out front." Ericka said.

Millie said, "That truck is your surprise; the driver said he'd be back in two weeks to pick the truck up."

"What's inside the truck and who sent it?" Ericka asked.

Millie handed her an envelope with her name on it, So Ericka tore open the envelope and read the note and then she pulled out jewelry from the envelope. It was gorgeous there was a diamond necklace with matching drop earrings and bracelet then there was two ring's that had diamonds in them, one was Lulu class ring where she graduated from the college of design school and the other was the ring, she wore all the time for the baby she lost due to her illness, it had a diamond with sapphires surrounding it then little angels wings on each side. I remember she told me once that I reminded her of what she could be and that one day she would make sure that I knew how much I meant to her as a friend.

Millie said, "That's beautiful and as you wear that ring you know she's always with you." and handed Ericka the keys to the truck. Ericka called Claire to come over before she opened the truck. Claire, Millie, and Ericka unlocked the truck and open the back and there was all of Lulu sewing machine and notions and file cabinets of dress designs that never got made due to her illness and there were thousands of yards of material and fabrics and notions it was just amazing the stuff in that truck. There was too much to go through it all, it was at 28-foot U-Haul, and it was filled full. Saturday after the furniture comes then we can unload the truck. I helped Millie make omelets, hash brown casserole, bacon, sausage, scones, and honey butter for dinner. I helped her set the table and I let Nancy know that dinner was ready, she said that Millie didn't have to cook for them, they could go out or order in, but I told them that we'd be happy to have them for dinner. Everyone ate good and George raved about the breakfast casserole, then as everyone went their separate ways, Millie said that Nancy said that they weren't going tomorrow night, they didn't bring any dress clothes, so they were staying here. Friday morning, I asked Millie to bring Nancy and Amanda down to the bridal shop that I wanted them to see it and I took Samantha with me to hang out with me at work.

I had Sarah's dress done and she was coming in today to pick it up and I had a surprise for her. Sarah showed up around 10 and I showed her the remade dress and she loved it so. I had her try it on in case I needed to make any alterations, but it fit perfectly. Then I told her that I have a surprise for her, I knew her colors were peach and teal so I made Sarah's mom a dress for the wedding it was light coral with a light teal jacket in case she gets cold and I made it to fit her mom in the wheelchair so it was easy to put on or take off with little ease and I told her I used the picture that she gave me of her mom and her so if I need to do any alterations, just call me and I'll come to her. After we settled up, I gave her an envelope with $100.00 dollars as a wedding gift. She hugged me and she left the door open as she was leaving. Then I saw Millie getting out of her SUV and headed this way with Nancy and Amanda. I had already laid out several dresses for them to try on and I had a surprise for Millie. I had made her a tea length dress in sage green with the swing hem and a white jacket trimmed in sage green to match with a matching handbag.

"Hello Nancy, Amanda how do you like my shop? It's a bit messy but with me moving it's been a little hectic." Ericka said.

Amanda said, "I love it, look at all the beautiful dresses that you have."

Nancy smiled, "You look lovely today, Ericka, I love this place and you have a great location."

"Thank you I wanted you to see my place, I really want you to come tonight to the dinner, so I have pulled some dresses out for you to wear please." Ericka said.

"Oh, momma can we please, I really want to see Ericka get her award for saving Daddy." Amanda said.

"Only if you let us pay for them." Nancy said.

"It's my gift to you, you're so sweet and I feel like were family, growing up I didn't meet very many kind people but here I haven't met anyone that's bad." Ericka said.

"Ok" Nancy said, "let's do this."

"Yeah" Amanda said.

Millie said, "I'll sit here and give my opinion."

Ericka said, "No Millie, I have a dress for you to try on."

"I have a navy dress that I was planning on wearing." Millie said, "I don't want to be any trouble."

"Follow me ladies in each dressing room you'll find 4 or 5 dresses to try on and pick, then if I need to alter any of them I will, go ladies try them on." Ericka said then she turned to Millie, "I have a special dress for you, please try it and let me know what you think."

Millie walked out wearing the sage dress with the jacket over her arms she looked beautiful, I knew the color would be prefect for her.

"You look beautiful Millie, what do you think?" Ericka asked.

Millie smiled, "I love it, it fits prefect and I love the color and I love that it has a jacket in case I get cold, thank you Ericka." and Millie hugged her.

Nancy came out of her dressing room in a maroon color tea length with short sleeves with gold trim on the neckline and had a matching belt in gold and because Nancy being short it was almost a maxi length, but she looked beautiful.

Nancy said, "I really like this one, the red didn't feel right and the blue one was really loose, but I feel great in this one, what do you think?"

"I think you look beautiful and so that's your dress." Ericka said. Nancy loved Millie's dress and while they talked Amanda came out of the dressing room dressed in a cobalt mid length dress that was off the shoulder on one side and had the handkerchief hem that ran between tea length and maxi length. "I really like the way this make me feel." Amanda said.

"You look beautiful Amanda." Ericka said, "So you have your dress now, if you need shoes there are two boxes of new shoes to pick from. Good luck searching, everybody." Ericka said.

Then I told Millie "Besides shoes to go with your dress, I have you handbag."

After they were done, Millie took them back to the B&B then I called and checked on Claire then I locked up and headed home.

The dinner and award ceremony started at six, so Lucy came by at 3 to pick up Sam and she had Sherry with her. Sam kissed Ericka and then they left.

Ericka showered and put her under cloths on, polished her nails and did her makeup, put perfume on so that it would air dry before she put her dress on so it wouldn't damage the dress. Then she fixed her hair she curled it and pulled it up in a low bun in the back with a small bunch of flowers in the bun then she curled the front strands to hang down around her face but you could still see her earrings that she put on from lulu then she stepped into her dress and zipped it up, it only went just half way up her back and the low front had layer that hung down like the cowl neckline then she put her necklace on then her ring and bracelet. Looking into the mirror she looked like someone she had never seen before. Then she filled her handbag then went downstairs where Millie was dressed and ready and as we waited for George, who came in looking dapper then when Nancy walked in George eyes got big and said, "You look beautiful my dear."

Nancy said, "Thank you hon." and kissed him then she winked at me and Millie.

Amanda came down the stairs looking radiant in her dress, George said, "I don't think I have ever seen this many beautiful women in one room before. Amanda, you look stunning; you look like your mom at that age."

"Thank you, Daddy, you look great too" Amanda said.

I heard John SUV pull up and then I heard Ron's pull up behind him and I said, "Alright let's get going."

As we step out the front door John stop dead in his tracks he smiled and said, "You look beautiful ladies."

Ron said, "I have never seen you dressed up Millie, you look beautiful."

Ericka said, "Ron this is George, Nancy his wife and Amanda his daughter."

Ron said, "Nice to meet you, I'll be your driver tonight."

And he helped Nancy in with George then he asked Amanda, "Would like to sit up front with me?"

Amanda said, "Yes I'd love to, thank you for picking us up."

"It's my pleasure mam." Ron said.

"Call me Amanda please, may I call you Ron?" Amanda asked.

"Yes, Amanda I'd like that." Ron said.

John help Millie gets in the SUV, she said she could sit in the back, but I insisted she sit up front, then he helped me in and whispered, "You look beautiful and so sexy, I hope I can contain myself." and winked at her.

Ericka just laughed, "We better get going."

The night turned out great, we had a wonderful time, James asked Millie to dance, and John took pictures. Father Morris walked over to talk for a few minutes. Claire showed up looking beautiful in an orange evening dress. Dinner was delicious and John danced with her several times. I reminded him to dance with Millie and then I told Ron to dance with Millie at least once and I took pictures of her dancing with her boys. Ron danced most of the night with Amanda they seemed infatuated with each other, Nancy and George danced a few dances then they started the awards ceremony at 9 and they did the fire department first and handed out a lot of awards then they awarded Ericka the Hero award for Saving George's life and helping out with Samantha Jones and showing that all you have to do is look inside your heart and do what's right. Then the police went on after them and handed out so many awards for the good deeds that they do, the danger that they face every day, and they honored a falling officer. Then the last award was the HERO Award and they presented it to Ericka for saving George life and her help in apprehending a dangerous person and then they awarded her A Shield of life for being injured during a dangerous situation and saving the lives of Millie and Samantha. James had the honor of awarding Ericka this award. Then the dance started and went on till 1 am. We stayed another hour then James took Millie home and John offered George and Nancy a ride back so that Amanda and Ron could continue to dance. When we got back to Millie's, I helped George out while John helped Nancy out and we walked them in and said our goodnights, then John asked me if I'd like to go for a walk so Ericka said yes and they walked to town, all deck in in their dress cloths. They sat on a bench at the park and John looked into Ericka eyes and smiled "You look beautiful tonight but then you always do."

"Thank you, John you look, great too." Ericka said shuddering some.

"Are you cold?" John asked.

"No just nervous." Ericka said in a low voice.

"Why are you nervous?" John asked and Ericka just shook her head as if she didn't know.

"Ericka, I think I'm falling in love with you, I can't think or even work without you being on my mind all the time. I miss you and after we had one night of bliss, I thought we could continue with a relationship build toward our future. What do you think?" John asked.

Ericka said, "I don't believe in love, I think you mean sex."

"No, I mean love, with the little white house with the picket fence and flowers and children. I want a future with you and Samantha." John said almost pleadingly.

"I don't believe in fairy tales, and neither should you. You need to face the reality of life, people get married and have children then they desert them or beat them, choose drugs over them, I can't do that, I'm sorry but if you're looking for you happily ever after then you're looking at the wrong girl." Ericka said, "I'm tired, I'm going home and getting some sleep goodnight." and Ericka stood up and bent down and kissed John on his lips then turned and walked back to Millie's all by herself. She went upstairs and stripped off and crawled into her empty bed and just laid there thinking about John. She heard someone in the hallway and didn't think anything of it but then her door opened, and John stood there looking at her. He shut the door and walked over to her bed and sit down beside her, "If I can have you this way then it's better than not having you at all." and he pulled her into his arms, and she willingly went into his arms, and they made love all night he was gentle with her because of her injury but he also showed her how passionate love could be. They wore each other out and they would fall asleep in each other's arms then wake up and go again it. It was like they couldn't get enough of each other but by early morning they had passed out and slept till the sun shone through her window and even then, John reached for her, and she willingly went with him again and again. They fell back asleep and when Ericka woke, he was gone, and she felt all alone. She was sore and raw, and she showered and put on cotton shorts and a halter top and went downstairs to get coffee, it was almost noon and Millie was sitting at the table drinking her coffee and pushed me the plate of scones my way when I sat down. I winced when I sat, and Millie smiled, "I remember those days."

Ericka said, "I'm just sore from dancing last night."

Millie said, "Is that what you're calling it, I saw John when he tried to sneak out unnoticed."

Ericka said, "Its complicated, I have to go to the shop, they were supposed to bring me my furniture before noon, but they haven't called."

"They called, I walked up and knocked on your door, but John answered, and I told him. John acted like he just got there to check on you, but he was in the same clothes from last night, he didn't want to hear it." Millie said.

"We'll I had better get to the shop." and I groaned as I stood up.

Millie yelled for Ron to come here. Ericka asked, "Why is Ron here so early."

"He came to visit Amanda, there going out later today, then they're going to pick up the girls around four, then come back so you work on the shop but drive please." Millie said.

Ericka decided to walk and walk off this soreness, but it didn't work. By the time she got to the shop the furniture was delivered Claire was there along with two guys from church and John was there also. I said "Hi" to everyone and they put me in a chair to direct, where I wanted the furniture and after it was all places the guys brought up all the bedding and household goods that I bought and put in each room then Claire asked if I wanted the guys to unload the U-Haul, so I gave the keys to Claire, and she told them where to put everything. They had the U-Haul unloaded and put in several of the sewing rooms and storage area by four o'clock. I thanked everybody and I tried to give them money, but they wouldn't take it. Everyone left but me and John and we just sat there looking at each other.

Ericka said, "Thank you for coming down today."

John said, "No Problem," John paused, "Ericka I can't do last night again, I want more and if you're not willing to try then I'll be here if you need help, but I can't make love to you and pretend it doesn't matter because it does matter for me. I want a house fence and children and you're the first person that I have ever loved. I can't pretend it's nothing when it's something special to me because I love you, but I can see that you're more damaged than I am. I might move to flagstaff to put some space between us at least for now."

And John got up, walked over to Ericka, and kissed her on her forehead and walked out, the whole time he was talking she had tears running down her face and even though he saw them, she never asked him to stay.

Ericka made the beds up and put sheets, blankets, and towels away, then she bought Sam some new clothes and she put them in her dresser and hung up a few pictures she had bought for her room. Then she made her bed and put a few things away before moving to the kitchen area where she washed dishes and put away, then she put a cloth on the table and sat a vase of artificial flowers in the center then she locked up and slowly walked to Millie's but when she got there Ron was arguing with John about running away but John saw Ericka and said, "I'll call you later." and hopped in his SUV and left. Ron looked at me, "What happened between you too?"

"It's a long story and I don't want to talk about it." Ericka said and went in to see Millie who was at the table with tears in her eyes.

"I'm sorry Millie." Ericka said.

"Don't worry about it, John has to find his own way. He's wanted someone to love him for a long time, maybe he'll find that someone special in Flagstaff." Millie said sadly.

I packed up my clothes and Sam's things and loaded them into the moving truck and I had the rental car picked up last week so I might as well move everything in the truck even though it isn't very much. I was loading the truck when Ron walked over and said, "Ericka, I'm sorry it's none of my business, me and Amanda are taking Sherry to the zoo for a movie night and fireworks can Sam come with us, its early yet so we can walk around so they can see the polar bears and tigers then we'll eat dinner there and order popcorn and watch the movie, it's Lilo and Stitch #2. We can drop her off after the movie or bring her here if you want."

Ericka smiled, "She loves Lilo and Stitch just bring her by the apartment when you're done, thanks Ron."

After Ericka got everything loaded Millie gave her some homemade scones, lunch meat, stuff shells, cans of soup, bread, and peanut butter with jelly.

Millie told her, "Call if you need anything."

Ericka said, "I will, you do the same Millie, I'll miss you."

Millie hugged Ericka and Ericka teared up and left and went home.

When she got everything unloaded and put away, she felt alone but at peace, she finally found a home to call her own.

She ate dinner then she went downstairs and worked on Nora's dress, it was almost finished, I had finished her veil the other day and needed to get this dress done. Mary's dress was done and so were all the hats. Then she had the other dresses cut and pinned on the mannequins. With the way she's going she should have everything done in a few weeks early. It was already the end of July and Claire is leaving in a few days to go on an extended cruise with her friend.

Sammy loved her room and hanging out with her at work. Clair came by to say goodbye and they had lunch together one last time.

As the weeks flew by Samantha and I settled into our home, social services came by to inspect.

I got all of Lucy dresses done three weeks early, everyone had their final fitting, and I was done with that job. I was invited to the wedding, but I didn't RSVP. Ericka hadn't heard a word from John sense that on Saturday she moved, apparently, he went to fill a temporary position in flagstaff, and no one was sure when or if he was coming home. I never asked Millie about John, I didn't want to upset her since it was entirely my fault for him leaving.

As for the bridal shop Ericka didn't reopen it yet she had several jobs for wedding dresses and special occasion dresses that she was too busy to run both. In her spare time, she made clothes for Samantha and Sherry and had gotten a lot of orders for children clothes. School went back to the first of September, and she had several orders for school clothes.

On weekends she started revamping the older dresses that were at the shop and she had sold several wedding dresses she had redone and modernized.

I got Sam signed up for head start and she starts the first week of October when she turns four the 2nd, I asked her if she wanted a party and she said she wanted a princess party. I have gotten to know a lot of women, that have children Sam's age, so I invited their kids to Sam's party, but I told each mom what all she has been through so that we could keep an eye on everything. I made a princess dress for Samantha, and I made Princess aprons for all the other girls, and I made vests for the boys that look like prince's, I made them all hats to match each apron and vest. I asked Millie to help me cook and bake for the party. I cleaned out the big area up in front of the shop and a set it up as a castle theme and one of the moms, Cindy that has a little girl same age as Sam, she's a beautician so I asked her to do the girl's hair and nails for the party and her sister does makeup, so she was coming to do light makeup and face painting. We decided to do a father daughter princess parade and ball.

I was hoping John would be back and maybe be Sam's pretend father, but I haven't heard from him, and I miss him so much. I try to stay busy, so I don't think about him but at night when I'm all alone I remember him, his face, his touch, and the way he made me feel. I realized after he left that I did love him, but I was too afraid of what could happen, but then I didn't think about what could really happen, we could work, I've seen so many married couples and happy children that I want that, and I want that with John, but I don't know how to tell him plus I'm so afraid that he's moved on. Maybe I'll ask Millie about John tonight when I see her to go over the food for the party in two weeks. Sam and I walked down to Millie's in the afternoon so Sam could play with Sherry now that's Millie keeping her every day and so we could discuss the menu.

I was worn out by the time I got to Millie's, she seemed concerned about me being so tired lately, but I told her I was fine. We picked out the menu and what we were cooking and buying. Sherry and Sam were playing in the sunroom, so I asked Millie "Have you heard from John?"

"Yes, I talked with him last night, he's fine, his job ends next week but he's not sure what he's going to do or go." Millie said.

"Is he coming home to visit at least?" Ericka asked.

"He didn't say dear, but he did ask about you." Millie said, "I don't think he's over you."

"That makes two of us, Millie. I'm sorry but I miss him so much, and I know it's my fault he left, but I was just so afraid of what could happen, I never thought about what if it worked out. Sam asks about Uncle John almost every night after she says her prayers, she always remembers to include him." Ericka said almost teary eyed then Ericka said, "Millie excuses me." and went running to the bathroom to throw up. This has happened often sense her knife injury, Millie came in and check on her, "I'm fine I'm getting used to it at least, I'm keeping my weight off after I eat." and Ericka laughed.

"I think you need to go back to that doctor and get a check-up you've been doing this for months now and you've lost weight." Millie said.

"I'm fine but after things settle down after Sam starts head start then I'll make an appointment I promise." Ericka said.

After they got back to the kitchen table Ericka asked, "Millie do you think John would come to Sam's party and be her pretend dad for her parade and dance?"

"I don't know Ericka if that would be fair to ask him to do that." Millie said, "But I'll ask him, just don't tell Sam and don't get your hopes up, Ok."

"Ok thanks Millie, I had better get back home and get more work done." Ericka said.

Millie said, "Why not leave Sam here to play and I'll have Ron drop her off after dinner tonight."

"Are you sure, I don't want to be any trouble, I've caused enough already." Ericka said.

"Your fine dear and Sherry gets lonely here by herself, hopefully when head start starts next month the girls will be in the same room." Millie said.

"I hope so." Ericka said, "But if not, they will be on the same bus at least."

Ericka went home and after she got there, she laid down on the couch for a few minutes and fell asleep and woke up at four thirty. She hopped up and went downstairs and started cleaning the small back room with all the

Black Box Company dresses. After talking to the professor, he invented the Black Box Company specifically for Lulu dresses and after her diagnosis, he shut the company down. As I opened box after box there were beautiful, exquisite designs in each box, all one of a kind. I called Professor Lyons and told him what we had found and asked him what he wanted me to do and he said they were mine I could do anything I wanted so I asked him if he was ok if I auction them off for a charity to help children of parents with drug abuse and we could call it Lulu children and he said that he loved that ideal and he knew Lulu would have too. So, after I got off the phone, I unpacked all of the boxes and there were over 300 dresses so now all I have to do is find out how to make a charity, but I'll do that tomorrow. I'm exhausted and Sam will be home soon. As I came out of the back room the phone was ringing, it was Millie. Sherry's staying the night and wanted Sam to stay and asked if it was ok, so I said yes, and Millie said she she'd have Sam call me before they go to bed. So, I went upstairs and fixed a plate of fruit and cheese to snack on and watch the news. I must have dozed off because the next thing I remember it was 6 in the morning and I was feeling sick and cramping so I took Tylenol and crawled into bed I slept on and off for a few hours then I called Millie and told her I was sick so she said not to worry about Sam and call if I need anything as the day went on I got feeling worst, Claire called to check on me and Sam and told me about her cruise. She asked me if I'd gone to the doctor yet, but I told her no and I told her how I was feeling today she said to go to the ER, but I told her I was too sick to drive and that I'd be better by tomorrow. After I got off the phone, I went downstairs and as the pain went through me, I lost my footing and tumbled down the stairs hitting my head on the railing and fell into darkness.

Claire was worried about Ericka so she called Millie and told her how bad Ericka was feeling and that when she suggested that she go to the ER, but Ericka said she couldn't drive because of the pain being so bad. Millie said she would send Ron to check on her and let her know what's going on. Millie called Ericka and didn't get an answer so she called Ron and asked if he could go check on Ericka, she was sick and not answering her phone and Millie didn't want to take the girls and upset them so he said he would. Just as soon as Ron hung up, John called, and he told John he'd call him back later he had to go check on Ericka because she's sick and not answering her phone.

Ron arrived at the shop and knocked on the apartment door but got no answer, so he went to the shop door and went in and saw Ericka on the floor at the bottom of the steps she had blood coming from a cut on her head and she felt cold and clammy, so he called 911 and the fire truck showed first then the ambulance came a few minutes behind them. They tried to get her to wake up but got no response, so they started CPR and after they got a pulse, they transported her immediately. Ron called Millie and told her that he was going to the hospital with her and that he would call and let her know what was going on. Ron didn't go into detail about how bad Ericka looked.

Millie called John and told him that, "Ron found Ericka at the bottom of the stairs and called an ambulance. I'm afraid it's bad, he said he was following her to the hospital." Millie said, "John you know how Ron talks when he doesn't want you to worry that's how he was talking." John said, "I'm on the way to the hospital."

Millie said, "Your hours away."

John said, "I called Ron because I'm on the way home and I was going to spend the night with him, I'm just about 15 minutes from town now, I'll call you later." and hung up.

Ericka came to the ambulance groaning in pain, the EMS worker asked where she hurt, and she said everywhere especially in her stomach. They put an IV in and put her on a heart monitor and bandaged her head. As soon as they pulled up to the ER doors, there was a team of doctors and nurses there that took over and rushed her into a room and examined her. Ron checked in and they didn't know anything yet. And almost an hour later the doctor came out to see if anyone was there for Ericka Mann. Ron stood up, "I am, how is she, doctor?"

"Are you family sir?" the doctor asked.

Ron said, "Yes I'm her cousin and we have no other family except her daughter that's almost four."

"We have her somewhat stable, she has stitches in her head and a concussion and were monitoring the baby, but she may lose it. She coded in the ambulance, and we are monitoring her heart. We're doing our best, as soon as we get a bed in ICU, we'll transfer her. I'll have the nurse come out and let you know when that will be." the ER Doctor said.

Ron asked. "Can I see her?"

"It will be a while, I'll have the nurse come get you as soon as we can." and the doctor walked away.

Ron went to call Millie and suddenly John was rushing through the door towards him, "How is Ericka, what happened to her?"

Ron said, "Let's sit down and I'll tell you everything the doctor just told me."

Ron told John everything the doctor said, John was shocked that Ericka was pregnant and didn't tell him and that she Coded, and she could die, he could lose her forever. Ron went and called Millie and filled her in and told her not to tell the girls anything yet until they knew more. It was after eight o'clock before they got a room for Ericka, and she wasn't stable enough to have visitors, the doctor said she was in and out of consciousness the whole time. The doctor came out and said, "We're transferring her to CCU because of her heart and we think that she has a heart infection from the stabbing back in July and its doing some major damage."

"She's too unstable for visitors so you might as well go home and come back tomorrow but if something happens through the night, then the nurse will call." said the ER doctor.

John and Ron both said, "We're staying."

"Ok there's a waiting room outside of CCU for you two to stay and I'll let her nurse know that you will be there tonight." the doctor said.

It was a long night, and the nurse came out around five and said that Ericka woke up and she's responding to the antibiotics, but she had a rough road ahead of her.

John asked, "Can I see her?"

"Not until the doctor comes in and he's usually here anytime between now and eight. I'll let him know you're here so he can come and talk with you." she said and went back to CCU.

The waiting room attendant said that we needed to go to consult room # 2 and Dr. Rabin would see us.

The doctor introduced himself and explained that he was the heart specialist and that "The bloodwork showed that Ericka does have a heart infection most likely from her recent stabbing and a blood infection usually mask another symptom's, so it's not easily caught until it's too late but that Ericka responding to the antibiotic's. There has been some damage to her heart, but they think she's over the worst part of it for now. But her infection is really bad for someone that's having a baby, so we don't know yet if she'll carry the baby or not. We just have to watch her and see. When I talked with her this morning, she didn't even know that she was pregnant. Visiting hours are from 11 am to 8 pm for 15 minutes each time, but she needs to stay calm, and we have her sedated for now and we're watching her closely" and the doctor left them sitting there in shock.

Ron looked at John, "She didn't know she was pregnant so, she didn't lie or not tell you."

John said, "I know but what happens now?"

"We'll take one day at a time, Ok." Ron said, "I'm going to Millie's and let her know everything and shower and clean up and visit with the girls, I'll be back later this evening. Will you be ok by yourself?"

"Yes, I'm fine just trying to process all of this information, I'm just glad Ericka is going to be fine." John said.

John went in and sat with Ericka at 11 and she was sleeping so he didn't wake her he just sat there and held her hand and watched her sleep.

Nurse Ellen came in and asked, "How's she doing has she woke up?"

"No, I didn't want to wake her, she seems comfortable, and I figured she needs her sleep." John said.

"Yes, especially after this morning, we had to sedate her, so she'll probably sleep most of the afternoon." the nurse said.

"Why what happened this morning" John asked.

"She got upset after the doctor left and cried and made herself sick, do you need anything?" Nurse Ellen asked.

"No, do I have to leave, or can I stay and sit with her just in case she wakes up." John asked.

"Yes, you can stay, the doctor wants her to start eating so he put her on a soft diet, so lunch comes at 12:30 and we'll try to wake her then. If you want coffee or soda just let us know and we'll bring it in to you." and the nurse walked out.

The nurse came in and brought Ericka her lunch and she tried to wake Ericka up she stirred some, but she didn't fully wake so the nurse said they would try again later.

John was sitting in a recliner beside Ericka and had dozed off holding her hand.

Ericka woke up, everything was fuzzy at first then she remembered the doctor this morning, she went to move in the bed to get more comfortable when she realized that John was sitting by her bed asleep. She carefully scooted up trying not to wake John, he must know about the baby she thought, what he must think of me now, but I couldn't tell him something that I didn't even know. John moved and opened his eyes and looked into my eyes.

"Your awake, how do you feel?" John asked slowly.

"I'm not sure, I don't understand what exactly happened to me to wind up in the hospital and then finding out about the baby. How can I be so stupid and not know that I was pregnant, it doesn't make sense to me." Ericka said with tears running down her face, "I'm so sorry John, I didn't know, I'm sorry."

John gathered her in his arms and held her, "It's ok we'll get through this but first we have to get you healthy and everything else will just fall into place, I promise you."

John pushed the nurses call button and when the nurse came in, she asked, "What do you need? Oh, good your awake, how do you feel?"

"Tired and I hurt all over." Ericka said.

"Let's get your vitals then I'll get you something for pain." and Ericka's vitals were good, and the nurse went to get her antibiotic and Tylenol. Dinner came and Ericka ate part of her food then she napped through the evening. Millie and Ron came up to visit and Ron took John down to the cafeteria to eat and Millie stayed with Ericka.

"How's Samantha doing?" Ericka asked.

Millie said, "She misses you, but I told her you'd be home soon."

Ericka said, "Millie I'm so sorry I didn't know about the baby, I'm so stupid I didn't even realize I was sick."

Millie said, "It's fine, the good thing is that they caught your infection before it did too much damage and that baby is doing fine. What have you decided about the baby?"

"John knows and we'll figure it out once I'm home, even though it was a shock to find out, I'm happy about this baby and I'm happy to see John, I really missed him." Ericka said.

Millie said, "Sounds like love to me, maybe love is real and you to have found it wouldn't that be a miracle."

Ericka smiled, "I'd like to believe that, but we haven't talked about everything yet so I'm being cautions."

They moved Ericka to a PCU the next day and after two days then to a regular room for the rest of the week, then doctors released her, and John took her home to Millie's. Millie had the girls there and had made a big family dinner. Samantha was glad to have her mom home and she asked if they were going home to sleep tonight and when Ericka said "Yes" Samantha jumped for joy she said she missed her bed and home.

After dinner, Millie fixed her food to take home, so she didn't have to cook tomorrow then John took Ericka and Samantha home. After she got home and settled on the couch, John had Sam give her mom a kiss night and he helped Sam get ready and tucked her in and kissed her on the forehead, "I love you sweetie, goodnight." John said, Sam gave him a hug and said, "I love you too, night."

John joined Ericka on the couch, and he sat beside her and asked, "How are you feeling?"

Ericka said, "Exhausted, but glad to be home."

"We'll you have to take it easy for the next few weeks hopefully you'll regain your strength in no time." John said.

"I can't take it easy, I have too much to do, Sam starts head start next Monday, her birthday is Friday, and her princess party is this Saturday that's only five days away." Ericka said.

"I'll help you with the party and getting Sam ready for Monday." John said, "It can't be that hard to get one little girl ready for school."

"She needs clothes and shoes and a backpack and Friday she has her physical and shots, plus I have to finish decorating the party room and coordinate the help for the parade and dance. Which reminds me, it's a father daughter dance, can you be Sam's date? I hate to throw that at you with everything that's happened, but I don't have anyone else that Sam knows or would even want. Ron offered to be her and Sherry's date, but I don't want to take away from Sherry." Ericka said slightly out of breath.

"Slow down, we can do this together and you still take it easy, ok." John said, "Now I think you need to get some sleep so go get in bed, I'll fix you a cup of tea and a slice of cake and bring it to you."

"Ok thanks John." Ericka said, and she went to her bedroom and put on her night gown and got ready for bed then she crawled into her bed, and it felt so nice to be home. After she got comfortable, she wondered when she and John were going to talk about the baby and the future, and she laid there fantasizing about them being a big happy family and she dozed off.

John fixed Ericka a cup of tea and a sliced of coconut cake and he put a rose on the plate with a chocolate heart and a ring box opened showing a diamond engagement ring. He carried the tray into her room, and she was sound asleep, he sat down and looked at her, she was so beautiful, and he loved her so much, he hoped that maybe she wouldn't be afraid of marriage now that she's having a baby. I guess we'll have to wait till tomorrow to see. John slept on the couch and got up several times checking on Ericka and Sam, he was up and had breakfast done by eight o'clock and Sam came into the kitchen, so John fixed her a plate and while she ate, he went to check on Ericka.

She wasn't in bed, and she wasn't in the bathroom, so he asked Sam, "Have you seen your mom? "

"No, she's probably downstairs." Sam said with a mouth full of scrambled eggs.

John went downstairs and sure enough Ericka was downstairs working. John asked, "What are you doing?"

Ericka looked up surprised, "Sorry I thought I'd get this done and back in bed before you woke up."

"Ericka you're supposed to be taking it easy, not building a castle." John said a little frustrated.

"I don't have that much left to do and I need to get it done so that I can finish decorating today." Ericka said stubbornly.

"Come up and eat, then I'll help you, ok." John said, trying not to upset her.

Ericka smiled, "Ok I'll come." John helped her up and they went back upstairs Ericka ate breakfast and drank her coffee and Millie and Sherry came over to check on everybody and they took Sam home with them for the day. John and Ericka worked on finishing the castle wall and decorating the entire room then Ericka worked in a small room setting it up for the girls to get their hair make-up and nails done and John set up the walk-in closet for the girls to get dressed for the party, parade, and dance then the cleaned the lounge area for all the food. They went upstairs around 5 and John heated leftovers up for their dinner and while they ate John asked questions about who was doing what and when and Ericka had it all in her head.

Then John asked Ericka, "What are you getting Sam as a gift for her birthday?"

Ericka looked up in shock, "I don't know, I've been working on her party, I forgot to get her anything."

John said, "Friday when we take her to the doctor, we can take her out to lunch and Millie said that she was making her a birthday cake and dinner Friday evening so what does she want for her birthday?"

"All she said was a princess party, I had plan on getting her an American baby doll, but I've been so busy, I haven't got out to get one." Ericka said.

"What about that box of dolls that was in the closet downstairs is that for her birthday?" John asked.

"No not really, I have invited 12 girls and six boys so I got each girl a princess doll and each boy a plastic sword set so they would have something to take home besides the goody bags of candy and trinkets." Ericka explained.

"What if we call Millie and have her keep Sam and if you're not too tired we can go shopping tonight" John offered.

"I'm exhausted, but I do want to go shopping so let me call Millie, you finish eating then we can go." Ericka said.

John said, "You need to finish eating too then we'll go, ok."

Ericka said, "Ok" and gobbled her food down and called Millie.

John took Ericka to Centertown Mall shopping, and they went to several stores and Ericka found the American girl twins babies she picked the dark hair twins and pick out a double stroller and several outfits for the dolls and doll cribs and changing table. Then John got Sam a small pink bicycle with training wheels and a white basket on front and he picked out a light grey teddy bear with a big pink bow around its neck to ride in the basket. Then after we both checked out then we shopped and bought Sam clothes, shoes, and a backpack for school. When they were done the SUV was packed full. Millie called to ask if Sam could stay the night with Sherry, so Ericka agreed.

Ericka went into Walmart and bought more party favors and a crystal tiara, a small diamond necklace, earring and bracelet in the children jewelry and got them for Sam. After paying John asked if Ericka, "Are you hungry?"

Ericka said, "Yes I could eat." so John stopped at an Applebee's, and they got seated and ordered sandwiches and drinks. They sat there talking and Ericka realized that John was looking at her and not saying a word.

"Is something the matter do I have food on my face?" Ericka asked.

"No, I was just looking at how beautiful you are and that I love you. I don't want to upset you, but I think it's about time we talk about what happened and about the baby." John said.

"I think we need to talk also but could we put it off just tell we get through this weekend. Sam's party is the most important thing right now and I'm not going anywhere so come Sunday you have my full attention, I promise." Ericka said.

"Ok then Sunday we will talk." John said sounding disappointed.

Ericka smiled and said "John, I love you too and we will figure this out, I promise."

After they got back to the shop, they unloaded everything inside where the party was going to be so while John put the bicycle together Ericka wrapped Sam's gifts. They finally got upstairs after 2 am and Ericka went to bed, and John slept on the couch.

Wednesday and Thursday were hectic, but they had everything done and ready by Thursday night. Friday morning Ericka helped Sam get her bath and put her jeans and a birthday shirt on that said, "Everyone Kiss the birthday Girl" after breakfast they went to the health department for her shots then to the doctor for her physical then to lunch at chucky cheese. Then we took her to the park to play and then to Millie's for dinner and cake and ice cream. Millie got her Barbie doll and clothes, and Ron and Sherry got her the Barbie house but by eight o'clock Sam was wiped out and so was Ericka. John and Ericka decided to give Sam her gifts to her in the morning, so when they got home John tucked Sam in bed and Ericka sat in the recliner and fell asleep. John went downstairs and double checked that everything was done then he came upstairs and woke Ericka up and talked her into going to bed. Ericka changed into her gown and noticed where her scar was that it was red and tender, but she thought that it could wait till Monday, so she didn't say anything to anyone.

Saturday was the big day, Ericka got up early and cooked breakfast. John woke up to the smell of coffee and bacon, Sam woke up excited about her party and after she ate, John and Ericka gave Sam her gifts and she loved them.

As she played through the afternoon, Ericka coordinated with the other volunteers and got the party going. Ericka showed Cindy the room to do the girls hair and there was a nail station and a makeup station. Cindy brought her sister Carly to do nails and Trina that works with Cindy to do makeup. Millie was helping Robin, one of the other moms, to help the girls get dressed and Ron was helping the boys get their shirts and swords on. The food was ordered from Jacks pizza and subs and the bakery made the cake, cupcakes, cookies and all the sweets. By the time the party was starting Ericka was in some serious pain, but everything went smoothly. The chief of police James led the parade down the block and up by the park the local newspaper took pictures and one of the fathers had a photography studio, so he took pictures of each child free then after the parade they ate then the dance started. John danced with Sam, and they had a great time then all the kids danced everywhere. The kids had a really good time and so did their parents. It was going on at eleven when the last of everyone left except Millie, Ron, and Sherry.

Ericka asked Millie, "Can you take Sam home with you?"

"Yes of course, I take it that you and John need time alone." Millie asked smiling.

Ericka said, "Yes we do, but not tonight, I need to go to the hospital."

Millie said, "Oh my, are you ok? is it the baby?"

"No, I don't think so." Ericka said and raised her blouse to show Millie how red and angry her scar looked.

Millie said, "Oh My Gosh you should have gone to the hospital immediately, why did you wait?"

"I didn't want to disappoint Sam." Ericka said, "But it hurts really badly so I need to go but I hate to show John."

Millie said, "John needs to know, now unless you want what happened last time to happen again, this time you need to tell him."

"No, I don't so if you'll take Sam then I'll have John take me, I just don't want to scare or upset Sam." Ericka said.

"I understand and I'll get Sam so you can get going, tomorrow we'll clean up ok." Millie said.

Millie went and talked with Ron and asked Sam to come home with her and stay the night with Sherry so after they left, John walked over, "I'm surprise you let her spend the night tonight."

Ericka said, "I need to go somewhere, and I can't take Sam with me, so I asked Millie to take her."

"Where do you need to go at this hour?" John asked.

Ericka lifted up her blouse and said, "Hospital."

"Good lord why didn't you say something?" John asked franticly.

"I didn't want to mess up Sam's party, can we go now before I start crying from pain." Ericka asked.

John rushed her to the hospital, and they admitted her and scheduled surgery to open the scar and clean it out first thing in the morning. The doctor assured Ericka that the procedure wouldn't hurt the baby, he was going to give her an epidural and numb her, but she'd be awake the whole time, but she wouldn't have any pain. They took her to surgery John kissed her and whispered to her, "I love you and I'll be here when you get back."

She was groggy and sleepy, she remembers part of the procedure, but she dozed on and off through it, which the doctor said is normal. She returned to her room and John was there and he kissed her and asked how she felt, she said" I'm feeling some pain." John went out to the desk and told the nurse. John sat by her bed looking at her sleeping then they gave her pain medicine and she had gone to sleep.

Ericka woke up later and saw John sitting by her bed watching over her, she reached out and held his hand "John, are you mad at me?" Ericka asked.

"No" John said, "But you need to learn that it's ok to put yourself first sometimes especially when it's your life on the line."

"I just didn't want to disappoint Sam and her friends and you." Ericka said.

"I wouldn't have been disappointed in you. I love you Ericka, I would have had Ron and Millie take over and got you help." John said.

"John, I love you too, but I'm scared what if I let you and Sam down like our parents let us down. I just don't know what to do as a mom or anything else, what if I turn out like my mom." Ericka said with tears in her eyes.

"You won't, you proved that when you step up and took Sam into your life and you are a great mom to her, and you'll be a great mom to our baby." John said.

"I'm afraid, what if I was so bad, that why my mom and dad did drugs." Ericka said.

John said, "Drugs is like a disease like alcoholism, and it controls everything and yes it destroys lives and family's but it's not your fault that your parents did drugs and abandon you. That was their choice to do drugs, not yours, you were just a child, we all were, and it wrecked our lives but we can't let it control how we live and feel." John said, holding Ericka.

Ericka dozed off through the afternoon and woke up and ate some potato soup for dinner. John called the nurse for more pain medicine for Ericka. She slept until six that morning then they came in and did her bloodwork.

Ericka woke for breakfast and saw flowers everywhere in her room, there were red roses, white lilies, carnations and beautiful mixed bouquets on her tables and nightstand. John was sitting in the recliner asleep looking so handsome, but he looked really tired.

Ericka laid there trying not to move much in case her incision started hurting the nurse came in and saw her awake, but Ericka pointed to John sleeping, so the nurse whispered, "How are you feeling, any pain?"

Ericka said, "A little but I'm thirsty can I have some water?"

"Yes, I'll go get you some and your doctors on this floor, so he'll be in to check on you?" the nurse said and left.

John heard the door and woke, "Hey beautiful, how are you feeling?"

Ericka said, "I'm doing ok just thirsty the nurse went to get me water."

The doctor came in as John walked over to Ericka planning on giving her a kiss. The doctor said, "Kiss the girl, it won't hurt her it can only make her feel better." and laughs.

John smiled and said "Ok, I will" and he leaned over her rail and kissed her gently on the lips.

The doctor said, "Now that we have that out of the way, you did good in surgery we cleaned out your incision and there was a pocket of infection so we got it all cleaned and stitch it inside with dissolvable stitches and then we used staples for the outside so you'll have to come see me in 10 days to take out the staples, light duty for six weeks, got it any questions?"

"No sir, I promise I'll take it easy, I have sewing to do but that's easy work, thank you Doctor." Ericka said.

"You're welcome, I'll get you paperwork done, and you can get out of her shortly but if you have any problems or concerns you call me immediately Ok." the Doctor said.

John said, "Yes Sir, I'll make sure she follows all your orders."

John walked over to Ericka and smiled, "You'll be home in your bed this afternoon and I know a little girl who will be thrilled." and he bent over and kissed her.

Ericka smiled, "I can't wait, I miss Sam so much."

Just then there was a knock on her door and Millie and Sam walked in. Sam asked John to pick her up so she could kiss her mommy so he put Sam on the bed beside Ericka and Sam kissed her mommy and asked, "Can we take you home, Mommy?"

"I'm waiting on my paperwork, but I should be home around lunch time." Ericka said and hugged Sam really big.

"Yeah, Mommy coming home." Sam said.

Millie smiled, "Then we had better get out of here and will be waiting for you at home." and gave Ericka a hug and took Sam and went home.

It was after lunch before Ericka got out of the hospital then John took her home. Ericka asked the nurse if they could bring a cart up for the flowers and when they brought the cart up and all the flowers were on it, Ericka asked John, "I love your flowers but now that I'm going home would you mind if I give them to the nurses to distribute to other patients?"

"No, I think that's a wonderful idea." so when the orderly came to take Ericka out, John pushed the cart to the nurse's station and told them what Ericka said and the nurses came over and gave Ericka hugs then finally Ericka made it home.

John helped Ericka settle in into her pajamas and into bed, insisting she nap for a while and that he'd go get a few groceries and would be back when she woke up and that later this afternoon Millie would bring Sam home.

Ericka snuggled down and went to sleep, and John left the house to run errands. John hurried back after ordering flowers and food and cake to surprise Ericka when she woke. John check on Ericka who was sleeping peacefully and he had flowers and roses delivered so he placed everything where he wanted then he had a steak dinner delivered with a small cake that looked like a wedding cake and he put champagne on ice and he set the table with a beautiful red Rose China that he bought to give Ericka as a house warming gift but never got the chance to give it to her so he thought this was the perfect time.

John heard Ericka moving around so he went to check on her, "Need any help?" John asked.

Ericka smiled. "I'm going to the bathroom, I'm just moving slow but I'll get there."

"Are you hungry? I have lunch ready." John said.

"Yes, I am, I'll be there in a minute." Ericka said as she went into the bathroom.

When Ericka came out of the bathroom, John was there and held her robe for her and as she slipped into it John could smell her perfume that she had just put on.

"Mum, you smell good." and lean over and kissed her on the lips, she kissed him back and leaned into him and he wrapped his arms around her and as the kissed deepened passion ignited and John almost forgot about his plans so he pulled away and looked in her eyes and smiled, "You drive me crazy, I not sure I can keep my hands off you."

Ericka smiled, "I don't want you to stop, I love you and I need you so much."

John could see the passion in her eyes, "I'm afraid I'll hurt you maybe we should wait tell you'll all healed up."

"I don't want to wait unless you've changed your mind about us?" Ericka said nervously.

"Never, I loved you so much, I just don't want anything else to happen to you. You and Sam mean the world to me." John said, and he kissed her. "Now I had better get you fed and settled before Millie and Sam come, Ok."

Ericka said, "Ok I'm hungry and I can't wait to see Sam, today was her first day of school and I missed it. I hope she'll forgive me?"

John said, "Of course she will, she loves you and she missed you a lot."

John took Ericka by the hand and escorted her into her living room and Ericka eyes got big and filled with tears as she saw all the flowers everywhere and John lead her to the table where there were red roses in the middle with Crystal candle holders on each side and beautiful China and wine glasses and champagne.

Ericka looked at John, "You did all this for me?"

"I'd do anything for you, I love you, Ericka." John said.

"I love you too" Ericka said as John helps her sit down in her chair. John went and brought the food to the table and then he brought this tiny, beautiful wedding cake in and set it down by Ericka. On top of the cake was a beautiful ring box. Ericka eyes glimmered with tears and John got down on one knee and took Ericka's hand and he kissed her hand and smiled with tears in his eyes, "Will you marry me Ericka Mann, I love you and I'll never leave you or disappoint you, I promised to love you, Sam and the baby all my life and never let you down."

Ericka tears ran down her face and she shook her head yes as John slipped the ring on her finger.

Ericka said, "Yes I love you, I promise to never let you down and I'll always love you and our family."

And as John got up, Ericka jumped out of her chair and threw herself into his arms and they kissed.

They heard a knock at the door so Ericka sat down, and John said, "That will be Millie and Sam." and he went and let them in. Sam and Sherry came running in to see Ericka and she hugged both as they both we're talking about school and how much fun they had, and Millie asked the girls to show Ericka their pictures they made at school today, so they pulled out the papers and showed Ericka and John. As they complimented them, someone knocked on the door, so Millie went and let in Ron who bought candy and flowers to welcome Ericka home. Sherry and Sam hugged Ron then went to play in Sam's room.

Ron said, "I'm glad your home, we all missed you and I do I see something special going on here?" as Ron noticed the ring on Ericka's hand and pointed to it so Millie would see it. Millie squealed and jumped up and hugged John then Ericka "Congratulations" Millie said, "When are you telling the girls?"

Ericka said, "It just happened before you got here."

John said, "We can tell her tonight after dinner if that's ok?"

"Yes, that's good" Ericka said.

Ron said, "I'm taking Sherry home, that way you can get some rest, Ericka." and he kissed her on the cheek, "I'm so happy for you both." he went to get Sherry.

Millie hugged both of us and said, "I knew you two was meant to be together, I'll see you tomorrow." and Millie left smiling.

Sam joined us and we all three ate and Sam was fascinated with the cake, so after we had cake then John asked Sam, "Would it was ok if we got married and become a family."

Sam said, "Yes oh Yes, I'll have a mommy and daddy." Sam hugged both John and Ericka then John pulled out a ring box and took out this tiny ring and said, "This ring binds us as family will you be my daughter Sam?"

Sam said, "Yes, I love you Uncle John."

John said, "You can call me daddy if you want?"

"Can I mommy, please?" Sam asked.

"Yes, Sam you can call John daddy from now on if you want." Ericka said.

Sam jumped up and down with excitement and hugged both John and Ericka then after she finished her cake she went to play in her room.

Ericka said, "Thank you John for giving Sam a ring and making her part of this."

John said, "She is part of this, I love her as if she was my own child."

While John did the dishes and put everything away Ericka filled out the papers from school then she very carefully helped Sam get a bath and ready for bed. Sam got down on her knees and said her prayers, "Thank you God for giving me a mommy and daddy if you have time will you give them a baby, so I'll have a baby brother or sister please, thank you amen."

Ericka went back into the living room and told John want Sam asked God for and they laughed.

John said, "We can tell her whenever you want but we need to set a wedding date."

They went over all the dates and decided on a fall wedding, they picked November 10th and that puts Ericka right at four months pregnant. So, Ericka worked on the wedding details as the week went by and she got stronger and the following week she went, and they took her staples out and she told the doctor that she was getting married. John went back to work and things went back to normal. Ericka worked on the shop and decided to open it back up as a bridal shop. She was covered up with dress orders and the shop stayed busy.

She had John help set up a charity for Lulu dresses and she had several people wanting them for their fundraiser, so she sold them to each charity for a large price to put into her fund for women and children.

As the fund grew, she bought an old hotel and renovated it into a women's and children's shelter and help women start over from abuse and get them back on their feet. As she was going through Lulu dresses, she found a beautiful ivory wedding dress that Ericka fell in love with, so she called the professor and asked him if he would mind her wearing one of Lulu dresses and he told her that he would be honored for me to wear one.

I asked him if he would come to the wedding, and he said that he would be there. Ericka made a small ivory hat with a veil hanging off it and then she had Millie help her pick out fall flowers and fall colors and they had the wedding in Millie's back yard. The day of the wedding the professor came to see Ericka and asked her if she needed someone to walk her down the aisle, he would be honored to be that someone. Ericka accepted his offer and told him that he was the only man that showed her respect when she was in college and that it was like Lulu being there watching over her.

Ericka went to the doctor that Friday morning before her wedding on Saturday and they did the ultrasound and told her she was having a girl. She stopped at the jewelry shop and bought John a wedding gift; she bought him a silver ID bracelet with the stick figures, she had them put the man, woman and two little girls and then it said, "OUR FAMILY" under the stick people. Then she had the underside engraved "I'll always love you."

She saw John for a few minutes Friday afternoon then she and Sam went to stay at Millie's where the girls and Millie threw Ericka a bridal shower then Saturday morning, she got flowers from John then after breakfast they all had their nails done then their hair then they went back to Millie and got ready for her wedding Millie helped her in her dress and to get ready then the photographer showed up and took pictures of Ericka and the girls. Ericka didn't have a maid of honor she wanted to ask Claire, but she was out of town, so she decided on just having Sam and Sherry to do the ring bearer and flower girl. Ericka looked out and the back yard was decorated in yellow daisies and sunflowers, yellow gold and red leaves and it all looked so perfect. There was a knock at the door, so she said come in thinking it was Millie coming to help her get dressed but when the door opened it was Claire standing there smiling.

Ericka ran over to her and hugged her, "I missed you, I didn't know you was going to come you didn't answer my call or letter."

"I told Millie not to mention me coming in case I didn't make it in time but I'm here for you, I'm so happy for you." Claire said and she handed Ericka a small gift.

Ericka said, "Can I open it?"

"Yes, you can, Millie said she loaned you her pearl earrings, and the girls gave you blue ribbons to put in you bouquet, I know your dress is from Lulu and it's new, so I have a pearl and diamond necklace that's old and I want you to have it." Claire said.

Ericka opens the box and there was a beautiful pearl necklace with a teardrop diamond hanging on it. It was the most beautiful necklace that I had ever seen.

"It's beautiful Claire, thank you I'll take good care of it and get it back to you after the wedding." Ericka said.

"It's yours to keep, I have no one to pass it down to, I want you to have it." and Clair hugged Ericka.

"Thank you so much, I love you Claire and I'm so glad you're here for my wedding day." Ericka said, "Have you been back to the doctor has anything changed?"

"Yes, I went last week and I'm in remission and feel great." Claire said.

Ericka hugged her, "I'm so happy are you staying home now if you want to work something out with the shop, I'll work for you if you want."

"No, the shop still yours, I don't know what my plans are but I'm not coming back to work, I'm not done seeing the world yet." Claire said.

Millie and Claire helped her get dressed in her wedding gown and at two o'clock it was time to get this show on the road. Ericka came down the stairs and the Professor was waiting at the bottom, "You look beautiful Ericka, Lulu would be so proud of you, and you look beautiful in that dress."

"Thank you, Professor." Ericka said.

"You can call me Robert instead of Professor, Ericka I think of us as family. Lulu loved you and was so proud of you and I'm honored to walk you down the aisle." Robert said.

"Yes, I loved Lulu, she and you both treated me like I was someone and I wish I would have had a family like you to raise me." Ericka said.

The music started playing so that everyone would get seated so we went to the kitchen to watch out the window in the door to see everyone sitting then they started the wedding march so Robert open the door then Claire walked out as my maid of honor, the Sherry and Sam walked out side by side throwing rose pedals everywhere and Ron walked with them as Johns best man, then Robert took my arm and we walked down the aisle to where John was standing. Robert kissed me on the cheek and shook John hand and went to sit down and John took my hand, and we step in front of the priest and said our vowels.

The day was beautiful, and Ericka and John said their vowels and kissed after the giving of the rings and then John escorted Ericka down the aisle to Millie's side yard where the photographer took lots of pictures. The guest went to the other side of the yard where there was a tent with food, drink, dance floor and music. There was a DJ playing all kinds of music and there were tables and chairs for everyone to sit in to eat. Then John and Ericka joined the party, and they were the happiest couple and a terrific family. Even though they would have ups and downs like anyone else they vowed to be there for each other, tell the end of time of time and they were.

John opened his own attorney's office and Erica bridal shop grew into a huge success. They had a beautiful little girl named Amelia who they named after Millie, and a few years later Erica had twin boys named Robert after the professor and Joseph after Joe, Millies late husband. Erica had another little girl who she named Clarisse after Claire. They bought the B&B from Millie and lived there and raised their children there after Millie married James and when he retired from the police department, he and Millie went on a cruise and traveled around to the world. Ron and Amanda got married and had a son and daughter to go with Sherry and they all lived happily ever after.

THE END

About the Author

My name is Patty Bullock and I have been happily married to my husband Rodney for 40 years. We have four amazing grown sons but sadly we lost one son last April and it broke our hearts but the love of family and friends have got us through all the good times and bad. Family means everything to me and they are the reason I love to write stories. I have been writing sense I was a teenager, I loved reading and started writing stories about love, romance, and adventure. I have written on and off as I grew up, got married, had kids, and worked full time until I retired several years ago. This is my second book that I have published and I hope you enjoy it as much as I enjoyed writing it.

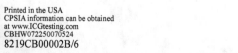

Printed in the USA
CPSIA information can be obtained
at www.ICGtesting.com
CBHW072250070524
8219CB00002B/6